Under Gemini

by

Linda Hope Lee

Under Gemini

COPYRIGHT © 2017 by Linda Hope Lee

Cover Art by *Kristian Norris*

The Wild Rose Press, Inc.
PO Box 708
Adams Basin, NY 14410-0708
Visit us at www.thewildrosepress.com

Publishing History
First Crimson Rose Edition, 2017
Print ISBN 978-1-5092-1262-0
Digital ISBN 978-1-5092-1263-7

Published in the United States of America

Dedication

To Pearl

Chapter One

Seattle, Washington

Johnny Stanton hunched over the steering wheel of his black SUV, waging war with the rain-slick road. Only a few more miles and he'd be home.

If he didn't pass out first.

Shortly after leaving Dooley's Bar and hitting the Interstate-5 freeway, wooziness overcame him. Now, on this uphill, winding road leading to Forest Glen, he could barely keep awake. Like being drunk in his pre-rehab days. But not quite. Something was different.

He'd had only coffee at Dooley's, but, damn, those jerks must've spiked it. Stupid of him to trust them. He made a fist and pounded the steering wheel.

But they'd said to meet him at the bar if he wanted to seal the deal. And he did. Oh, yeah. They told him he'd get his money next week.

Going into the bar meant leaving Aly in the back seat of the car. Under ordinary circumstances, he wouldn't have, but she'd been given a sedative at the hospital and fell asleep soon after he picked her up.

He risked a glance over his shoulder. Alyssa, his and Meg's beloved nine-year-old daughter, slept soundly. The cast on her right leg made a big lump under the red-and-blue plaid blanket he'd dug out of the trunk. Her blonde hair fanned out around her face, the sweet face of an angel. He was glad she was sleeping. The storm would scare her.

Again, he focused on the road ahead, listening to the rapid swish-swish of the windshield wipers. Only a couple more miles to the Forest Glen turnoff. He'd make it. He had to.

The urge to call Meg gripped him. He needed to touch base with someone, and his ex-wife was the one person he could trust. Then he remembered she had a date tonight. His gut twisted. He didn't like her being with another guy, even though they'd been divorced a year and he'd been seeing someone, too.

He'd call, anyway, and leave a message. He pulled one hand from the wheel and groped for his phone lying on the seat beside him. Found it. Managed to punch up his contact list and speed dial Meg's number.

The call went to voice mail. He waited through her message and heard the beep. "Meg, ish Johnny. Me 'n Aly er almosh home. Shesh fine." On impulse, he added, "I gotta tell ya somethin'." He hiccupped, and the bile rose in his throat. He swallowed it back down. "Ish under Gemini, Meg. 'Member that. Under Gemini."

Fumbling his thumb on the screen, he punched off the call. The phone slipped from his fingers and, with a soft thump, slid to the floor. His eyelids fluttered and then closed.

The tires hit gravel, jolting him wide-eyed. Where the hell had that curve come from? Pull the car to the left. No, to the right. Where's th' road? Damn blasted rain!

Out of nowhere, a guardrail appeared in front of the windshield. He jerked the steering wheel. Too late.

The SUV crashed through the rail and, like a plane taking off, soared into the stormy night.

The SUV arced into the canyon. Then, as Johnny watched in horror, it dove straight down toward the bottom. The car hit the ground, rolled over, and finally landed upside down against a Douglas fir.

Before the wheels stopped spinning, Johnny and Alyssa both were dead.

****

Megan Evans opened the door to her third floor, Queen Anne Hill apartment and stepped into the entryway. She shook out her umbrella, spraying drops of water onto the tiles, and then propped the umbrella against the wall.

Shivering, she hung her wet coat on the coat rack and hurried into the living room, intending to call Johnny and check on Aly. When she saw the blinking red light on the telephone, she felt a chill slither down her spine. The light looked ominous, somehow, flashing on-and-off in the semi-dark room.

Only one message, but the words were slurred and the voice unmistakably Johnny's. Meg gasped. Surely, he hadn't been drinking. After his three-month stay in rehab, he'd vowed he was through with alcohol.

Gripping the receiver, she replayed the message. Okay, Aly was fine, and they were almost home.

Then he added, "Ish under Gemini, Meg. 'Member that. Under Gemini.

She had no idea what he meant. But it wasn't important now. Johnny was drinking and driving—and their daughter was with him.

Sagging into a chair, Meg dialed Johnny's home number. After a couple rings, his voice mail clicked on.

She tapped her fingers on the table, waiting for the message to end. "Johnny, it's Meg. Call me." A call to Johnny's cell phone again switched her to voice mail. She left the same message she'd left on his home phone.

She checked her wristwatch. After ten. They should be home from the hospital by now. Aly should be tucked safely in bed. She phoned the hospital. The receptionist confirmed Aly's father had picked up their daughter that afternoon. No, she hadn't heard anything more from him.

Meg paced the room. Then, clutching her churning stomach, she slumped onto the sofa. Something was wrong, dreadfully wrong. She just knew it.

If only she hadn't gone out tonight, then Aly would have been with her, instead of with Johnny. But, last week, she agreed to a blind date arranged by a mutual friend. Then, two days ago, Aly fell while roller-skating and broke her leg. She was to be released from the hospital today. Meg wanted to pick up Aly and bring her home to the apartment, but Johnny insisted he would care for their child. They had joint custody, and this was his designated weekend.

Meg reluctantly went on her date. Bill Tate was a pleasant companion and the art gallery opening enjoyable, but no sparks flew between them. When he brought her home, neither mentioned getting together again.

Her street level doorbell buzzed. Gasping, she jumped up, ran to the apartment door, and pressed the intercom button. Maybe the caller was Johnny. Maybe he'd brought Aly here, after all. Her heart fluttered with anticipation.

"Ms. Evans?" a stranger's voice said.

"Yes?"

"I'm Officer Holmes, Seattle Police. May my partner and I come up?"

The police? Her mouth went dry. Why would they want to see her?

"Yes, of course." She pressed the release button for the outside door.

Moments later, she opened the apartment door to two grim-faced men in uniform. They flashed their identification cards. Numbly, she led them into the living room and motioned for them to sit. This scene wasn't real. This was a dream. Any time now, she'd wake up.

"Ms. Evans," Officer Holmes began with a shake of his head. "I'm afraid we have bad news…"

****

Two days later

His arms full of grocery bags, Eric Richards entered his apartment to the ringing of his cell phone. He kicked the door shut and rushed into the kitchen to set the bags on the counter. Then he pulled the phone from his shirt pocket just before the voice mail clicked on. "Eric here."

"Eric? It's Norrie."

"Norrie. How are you?" Guilt washed over him. He hadn't called her in weeks; he'd been busy with his software consulting business, not to mention the part-time investigative work he did for the FBI.

"I-I'm okay."

The hesitancy in her voice told him otherwise. "No, you're not. What's wrong?" He hoped she wasn't on drugs again. Norrie had spent six months in a drug rehab center. Since her release a few weeks ago, he'd seen her only once, when he took her to lunch. Shameful, after the promise he'd made her father.

"I-there's something going on here."

"At the res?" Norrie lived on the Nootlinga Indian Reservation, thirty miles north of Seattle. She was a blackjack dealer in their casino.

"Y-yes. Well, not here, but—"

"Tell me about it."

"Not over the phone. Can you come? Now? Please?"

A chill rippled down his spine. This was serious. He glanced at his wristwatch. Almost 9:00 p.m. "Of course, I can. Sit tight. I'll be there in an hour, tops."

Soon he was back in his truck, speeding along the I-5 freeway, his thoughts focused on Norrie. She was twenty-five and the only daughter of a good friend he'd had at the FBI, Max Vanderman.

Max had been killed two years ago during a drug bust in Tacoma. He'd been avid in his fight against drugs, not just because of his job, but for a personal reason as well. His wife and Norrie's mother, LaWannie, a full-blooded Nootlinga, was an alcoholic and drug addict who died an early death from cirrhosis of the liver. Max had done everything he could to help LaWannie kick her habits, but nothing worked.

Unfortunately, her mother's sad experience hadn't kept Norrie from following the same path. She experimented with drugs as a teenager and continued using into adulthood. Eric promised Max on his deathbed that he'd look out for Norrie. And he had—at first. He visited her frequently and eventually convinced her to enter rehab. But, he hadn't followed up very well after her release. He hoped he wouldn't be sorry now for his lapse.

On the outskirts of the reservation, Norrie's one-story frame house lay in darkness, as did the neighboring houses. He climbed the weathered steps to the wobbly porch, setting in motion a couple ferns in hanging baskets. The door was the old-fashioned kind with a window in the top half. A dark cloth covered the inside of the glass, with a faint light escaping around the edges.

Eric banged his fist on the door. He waited, tapping his toe on the rough wooden floorboards. No answer. He grabbed the doorknob, the metal cold under his fingers even on this warm May evening. The knob turned readily, and he burst inside. "Norrie! It's me, Eric!"

He dashed down the narrow hallway to the living room, stopping short in the doorway. "Oh, no!" Norrie lay sprawled on the worn burgundy sofa. One arm, flung over the side, was tied with a thick piece of rubber. A hypodermic needle lay on the carpet, directly under her fingers. Light from a shaded lamp shone on her face. Her skin was white, her lips blue.

His heart pounding, Eric ran to Norrie and knelt by her side. The slight rise and fall of her chest indicated she was still alive. "Norrie! Norrie!"

Her eyelids fluttered open. "Eric…"

"You're gonna be all right, baby." He leaned back and reached for his cell phone.

"W-wait."

He took out the phone, at the same time scanning the room to make sure she was alone. "What is it?"

"G-Gemini Island. D-don't f-forget. It's under

Gemini."

Whatever that means. "Okay, sure." He held up the phone and punched 9-1-1.

****

One month later

Meg placed the bouquet of roses in the sunken metal vase at the foot of the headstone. She ran a finger over one of the flower's silky pink petals. Pink was Aly's favorite color. Meg raised her tear-filled eyes and gazed at the stone's freshly engraved lettering. *Alyssa Marie Stanton.* Her beloved child was gone. How would she ever live without her?

Her gaze slid to the headstone next to Aly's, where Johnny's name and birth and death dates were recorded. The terrible accident that had taken his and Aly's lives had been ruled just that—an accident. He hadn't been drinking, as she'd feared. The autopsy revealed an over-the-counter cold medicine containing codeine had interacted with the drug he used to control his alcoholism.

Through a dry throat, Meg whispered a prayer for Aly and Johnny. Then she stood and, head bowed to muffle her sobs, stumbled across the cemetery lawn to her car.

On the drive home, through neighborhoods shaded with lofty fir and leafy maple trees, across the overpass spanning I-5, the unsettled feeling haunting her since that terrible night crept over her again.

Meg refused to believe Johnny would knowingly take a drug that would interfere with the one to control his alcoholism. Especially, he would never put their daughter at risk by driving while impaired. He loved Alyssa as much as Meg did. Add to that the mysterious message about Gemini. She told the police about the call and let them listen to Johnny's message.

They dismissed it as unimportant and declared the case closed.

But, like a wound that wouldn't heal, Meg believed the case was still open. Something was not right.

She lifted her chin and tightened her grip on the steering wheel. Somehow, she would find out the truth about Johnny's and Aly's deaths.

Back in her apartment, Meg paced the living room, wracking her brain for ideas. If only she knew what "under Gemini" meant. She'd gone to Johnny's house in Forest Glen—the house where they'd all lived together as a family—and searched through his belongings, but she had turned up nothing helpful.

In desperation, she sat at her computer, booted up a search engine, and typed in "Gemini." As expected, she found many references. Checking all of them would take hours, days, even. Yet, what other leads had she? Straightening her spine, she began her search.

Two hours and several cups of coffee later, a *Seattle Times* article about a Carl Miller, who owned Fortune Industries, caught her eye. The locally based company's interests spread overseas and ranged from timber to electronics. The article stated Miller owned Gemini Island, one of the San Juan Islands north of Washington State's mainland. A collector of Northwest Indian artifacts, Miller had built a museum there to house his collection.

Fortune Industries employed the accounting firm of Benson and Horton, for which Johnny had worked. She remembered the day he came home and told her he had been assigned the account. "It's the best thing that ever happened to me, Meg. Fortune Industries is big. Very big." Meg never knew how Johnny fared with his new assignment, because two months later, they separated and then divorced.

Now, she had a possible connection between Johnny and Fortune Industries and Gemini, an island in the San Juans. But she still didn't know for sure if that was the Gemini Johnny spoke of in his phone call. She blew out a deep breath and again placed her fingers on the keyboard. This time, she'd do a search on Fortune Industries. As she scanned their website, she spotted a Job Opportunities icon and clicked it. Nearly a hundred positions were listed, not surprising for such an extensive operation. She studied the list, stopping when she read: *Person needed to assist in cataloging large private collection of Northwest Indian artifacts. Museum experience helpful but not necessary. Must be willing to relocate.*

Meg's heart beat faster. Surely, this must refer to Carl Miller's own collection and his museum on Gemini Island.

Did the "must be willing to relocate" mean moving to the island? Leaving town would mean putting her freelance consulting business on hold. She was under contract to help several women clients develop their home-based businesses. Dropping out wouldn't be fair.

Leaving Seattle would be tough, too. She loved city life. She raised her gaze to the window. One reason she'd chosen this apartment on Queen Anne Hill was for the sweeping view of downtown Seattle. Her gaze roved over the forest of skyscrapers and came to rest on the famous landmark, the Space Needle, with its saucer top, which held a revolving restaurant. The surrounding

Seattle Center was a favorite place, and she spent many pleasant hours there visiting the shops and strolling the grounds.

How could she exchange her life in the city for life on a small remote island, even for a short while?

A knot formed in her stomach. She had no real choice. For her beloved Aly's sake, she must find out the truth behind the terrible accident that took her life. For her daughter, Meg would do anything. And for Johnny's sake, too. She harbored no anger toward him, only sadness.

The job on Gemini was a long shot with no guarantees, but she had to try. Meg picked up her phone and punched in Fortune Industries' number.

Chapter Two

"I tell you, Eric, there's nothin' we can hang onto here. The kid was a junkie. Pure and simple."

Junkie. Eric hadn't heard that term in a while. But, then, the speaker, his FBI boss, Howard Zefrelli, was an old-timer. Junkie was what they called drug addicts decades ago, when Howard patrolled the streets, before a promotion sent him upstairs to sit behind a desk.

They were in Howard's office now, on the sixteenth floor of Seattle's Logan Building. Howard sat behind his desk, while Eric occupied a straight chair across from him. One wall had a large, plate-glass window, but the cloudy day outside kept the office dark and gloomy.

Eric stuck out his chin. "Her name is Norrie Vanderman."

Howard gave a dismissive wave, and then ran his fingers through his sparse, white hair. "I know, I know. Max's kid."

"Yeah, Max's kid." His voice dropped a notch.

"I know you and Max were buddies. I know you promised to look out for her when Max died. But that still doesn't justify a Bureau investigation into her death. We've got nothin' we can legitimately stick our noses into."

Eric sat forward and spread his hands. "But she'd been in rehab. She wouldn't go back to drugs. I know she wouldn't. She promised me. Besides, she had a job dealing blackjack in the casino. She looked forward to moving off the res into a better place."

Howard raised a skeptical eyebrow. "You want statistics on how many kids go back to drugs after they've been in rehab?"

Eric shook his head. "No, never mind. But there was this Gemini thing—"

"Right. Run that by me again."

"When I found her, she mumbled, 'Gemini Island. Don't forget it's under Gemini.'" Memories of that night flooded his mind—the anguish, the helplessness he'd felt after waiting at the hospital for word of Norrie's condition, only to learn she hadn't survived. He'd peeled out of the hospital parking lot, driven aimlessly around, and finally ended up back at her house. With a vengeance, he'd searched the place, looking for something, anything, to help him understand what had happened.

"And the note you found later at her house said what?"

Howard's deep voice cut into Eric's thoughts. He shrugged. "Just 'Gemini Island.' I'm betting she was interrupted before she could finish."

"And from that you concluded Gemini Island must somehow be connected with the drug trade." Howard shook his head.

"Why is that far-fetched?" Eric held up a hand. "Canada is only a few miles north. We know those waters aren't carefully patrolled."

Howard leaned forward. "You're forgetting something. The island belongs to Carl Miller. He's very well thought of around here."

"But—"

"But you want me to send you up there to investigate these so-called connections you've put together? Hey, in case you didn't know, the terrorist alert has been raised. We got bigger things to go after than petty drug smuggling."

A sinking feeling invaded his stomach, and he threw up his hands. "Okay, fine. Don't send me to Gemini. Forget it." He stood, paced to the window, and looked down at Elliott Bay, where a tugboat hauling a long load of timber passed a green-and-white ferry headed for the Olympic Peninsula. He hardly noticed the water traffic, though, or the gray clouds drifting across the sky. He was too busy thinking about Norrie. She'd been on his mind constantly since that fateful night. He'd let her down. If he'd paid her more attention, checked up on her more often, maybe she'd still be alive today. Eric turned and faced his boss. "I want some time off."

Howard raised his eyebrows. "What for?"

"Personal business."

"I think I know what that is. No, Eric, we need you here."

Eric propped his hands on his hips. "Come on, Howard. You know I've got time coming. I haven't had a vacation in quite a while."

"You don't want time off for any vacation."

"No, you're right. Like I said, I have personal business."

Howard sat rigid in his chair, his eyes narrowed. Finally, he leaned back and crossed his arms over his ample belly. "Okay, leave granted. But I have a feeling I'll regret it."

Eric left Howard's office and took the elevator down one floor. Nodding to several co-workers along the way, he continued along the hallway to his office, not nearly as large as Howard's and lacking a view, but adequate for the amount of time he spent there. Winning over Howard, a notoriously tough boss, should have made him feel good. But it hadn't. All he felt was the same despair he'd wrestled with since the night he discovered Norrie lying on her living room sofa, hovering between life and death.

He had to find out the truth. He didn't believe for one minute she overdosed herself with drugs, as the investigating officers concluded.

Someone murdered Norrie, same as if they'd put a gun to her head and fired.

****

Meg stood on the top deck of the ferry, watching Puget Sound's Orcas Island change from a gray blob into a landmass with discernible trees and structures. With an area of about fifty-seven square miles and a population of over four thousand, Orcas was the largest island in the San Juan group. She would debark there. Someone from Gemini Island, which had no public ferry service, would pick her up and take her to her final destination.

A week had passed since she'd inquired about a job as cataloguer for Carl Miller's Northwest Indian artifacts. The call resulted in an interview with Miller's associate, Kent Gheller. He glanced at her resume, which included a brief stint as a volunteer for the Seattle Art Museum, and hired her on the spot. Miller had moved up the museum's opening date and was in a hurry to fill the position.

Without hesitation, Meg accepted the job. Thankfully, her clients understood when she turned them over to another home-business consultant. No one at Fortune Industries should connect her with Johnny Stanton, because she'd taken back her maiden name when they divorced. And, since Johnny had become a Fortune accountant after the separation, she'd never met any of the employees. She felt safe in her new venture.

Safe as far as having her identity discovered, anyway. What would happen after she reached the island kept her nerves on edge. She could be walking into a dangerous situation.

Minutes later, the ferry docked at Orcas. Wheeling her suitcase with a tote slung over her shoulder, Meg joined the other foot passengers and left the boat. Everyone soon drifted away, leaving her to wait in the covered pedestrian shelter for her contact from Gemini.

Although, she wasn't quite alone. A man wearing a backpack and with a canvas bag at his feet also waited. Sunlight picked up highlights in his thick, dark hair and gave a golden cast to his tanned profile.

He turned in her direction, and their gazes met.

She offered the hint of a smile and a brief nod. He nodded and smiled, too, and then they both looked away. Meg pursed her lips and tapped her foot, wishing her contact from Gemini would arrive.

At last, a man approached. In his twenties, he was short, solidly built, and had his black hair pulled into a ponytail. Olive skin and a round face with a flat nose suggested Northwest Indian ancestry. A leather vest hung open over a brown T-shirt, and the ragged hems of his jeans draped over scuffed work boots. When he reached the shelter, he stopped and looked first at Meg and then at her companion. "You the ones going to Gemini?"

The man waiting stepped forward. "I am. I'm Eric Richards."

"I'm going there, too," Meg said. "Megan Evans."

"Jones, here to pick ya up. Boat's at the marina." He thumbed over his shoulder to the docks. "Here, lemme take that." He nodded at Meg's suitcase and held out his hand.

"Thank you." Meg turned over the suitcase and fell into step behind him.

Eric Richards picked up his canvas bag and caught up to Meg. "Are you visiting the island? A friend of Carl's?"

"No. This is my first trip there. I've been hired to work on the artifacts for Carl's new museum."

He raised his eyebrows. "So have I. But I didn't know anyone else was coming on board.

"Me, neither." Meg clutched the strap of her tote. "Mr. Miller's assistant, Kent Gheller, hired me a week ago. He didn't mention there would be anyone else."

"I'm in the software biz, but Northwest native art is a special interest of mine. Carl hired me as a consultant."

"I'll be cataloging the collection."

"Then it looks like we'll be—"

"—Working together," they finished in unison.

Working together. Meg's shoulders tightened. She'd counted on having the workplace to herself. Now she'd have to share it with Eric Richards. How could she do her investigating with him around? Eric's frown told her he didn't like the situation any better than she did.

Jones led them down a ramp, past gasoline pumps and a bait house, to the boat docks, where sailboat masts swayed with the tide and colorful flags high on flagpoles waved in the breeze. He stopped beside a mid-size cabin cruiser with *Kawanti* painted on the hull. He lifted Meg's suitcase aboard, and then he and Eric climbed in.

Eric turned and held out his hand to Meg.

Grasping his hand, she stepped from the dock onto the boat. She should have thrown in the tote first, though, because its weight on one shoulder put her off balance. She ended up having Eric take both her arms and lift her aboard. As she was set down, her cheek brushed against his chest. "Sorry," she mumbled, pulling away.

"No problem. But you'd better sit and stay put. Could be a bumpy ride." He led her to the padded bench at the stern and then joined Jones, who perched in the captain's chair.

Meg sat and put her tote down beside her, glad to have some distance between her and Eric Richards.

They soon left the marina and headed into open waters. Sitting in the stern left her unprotected from the wind but able to take in the spectacular scenery. Not a cloud hung in the cerulean sky, where seagulls swooped and soared, their caws echoing over the water.

However, the islands commanded the most attention. All shapes and sizes, they were scattered as though tossed from a giant hand. Meg's research had revealed about four hundred and fifty islands made up the San Juans. Out of all those, only one truly interested her, and that was Gemini. In her mind, she heard Johnny's voice on her answering machine the night he died: "It's under Gemini, Meg. Remember that."

A shiver trickled down her spine. Was she about to find out what Johnny meant?

****

Feet planted apart, Eric stood beside Jones while he steered the boat. "How far's the island?"

Jones kept his gaze focused on the water. "Not far."

"You live on the island?"

"Most of the time.

Eric leaned closer. "You look familiar. Thought maybe I'd seen you somewhere." Actually, he was fishing to find out whether or not Jones was Nootlinga, as Norrie had been.

"Doubt it." Jones gripped the wheel and clamped his jaw shut.

Okay, so much for that. Eric turned away to gaze out the windshield, leaving the man to his task. He still couldn't believe his good luck. Once he'd been on official leave from the Bureau, everything fell neatly and quickly into place. An acquaintance that knew Eric only as a software consultant and not as an FBI agent introduced him to Carl Miller. They talked computer software programs until Eric changed the subject to Carl's Gemini Island museum, tossing out a few bits of knowledge of Northwest Indians he'd learned from his crash course in the subject.

Carl said he had some artifacts needing positive identification and asked if Eric would be interested.

And here he was, on his way to Gemini.

He hadn't counted on working with anyone else. He glanced at Megan Evans sitting in the back of the boat. In her early-thirties, she had thick, dark brown hair drawn into a ponytail. Large brown eyes and a softly rounded chin gave her a vulnerable look. An air of sadness surrounded her, too. Something bad had happened, and not long ago.

A sharp swerve of the boat caused him to adjust his footing and snapped him to attention. They had reached Gemini and were headed around to the far side, where a wide bay accommodated several docks and half a dozen boats of various sizes. At anchor sat a yacht large enough to navigate the ocean. Yep, old Carl had a few bucks, all right.

Jones cut the engine and eased the *Kawanti* into an empty spot at one of the docks.

While Eric helped Jones secure the lines, he noticed Meg carefully stepping off the boat. He considered lending a hand again, but decided not to. She appeared to be doing okay on her own. Besides, he'd been all too aware of his pulse spike when he lifted her aboard. He needed to put a lid on that. He was on a mission, and attraction was something he didn't need.

He refocused on tying up the boat, but the next time he glanced her way, he saw her watching him. Instead of looking away, she lifted her chin and met his gaze, as though issuing a challenge. A challenge to what, he didn't know, but he'd bet he'd find out soon enough.

Chapter Three

Meg followed Jones and Eric along the dock. Just before stepping onto the shore, she felt her heart skip a beat. Once she set foot on land, there'd be no going back. For better or worse, at least for the duration of her employment, she'd be stuck here on Gemini Island.

She looked back the way they had come. Orcas Island was no longer visible, and the mainland was miles farther away, as though it belonged to another world, another time. "I'm doing this for you, Aly, my love," she whispered. Then, taking a deep breath and straightening her shoulders, she stepped onto the island.

Jones led them up a sandy bank to a cluster of motorized golf carts painted blue with white canopies. He loaded their luggage onto the back seat. Meg squeezed into the remaining space, leaving Eric to sit with Jones.

"Gotta stop at Carl's first," Jones said. "Then I'll take you to where you're stayin'.

They started off along a narrow, paved road lined with ferns and wild rhododendrons. The flowers were in full bloom, ranging from white to pink to dark red. Tall lampposts with round globes promised illumination once the sun had set. Still, judging by the thick woods of hemlock, cedar, and fir, the island after dark would be inky black.

At the far end of the island a tall peak towered

above the trees. She leaned forward and pointed. "Jones, is that a mountain over there?"

"Yeah," Jones said over his shoulder. "That's where the satellite dish is. We got everything here, TV, telephone, Wi-Fi."

"Does the mountain have a name?"

"Mt. Gemini, same as the island.

Meg slumped against the seat. "It's under Gemini," Johnny had said. But now there were two Geminis—the mountain and the island itself. Which one had he meant?

Moments later, they approached Carl Miller's home. Meg stared at the two-story building. Even though she knew he was wealthy, she hadn't expected such an elegant residence on this remote island. Several of the upper story rooms had balconies. A stone façade around the lower level gave the house a sturdy, solid look, while large windows added a light, airy touch. In front stood three totems painted in the traditional Northwest Indian colors of red, blue, and black.

Jones pulled the cart to a stop. "Gotta get the keys to your cottages from Laureen. You might as well come in and meet her."

Meg followed Eric and Jones up a stone walkway lined with ferns to large double doors carved with Indian designs. Jones pushed open one door, and they stepped into a spacious, sky-lighted entry. Soft burbling came from a pool where water cascaded over round, polished stones. Potted plants and several small totems added warmth and color to the setting.

Footsteps sounded on the marble floor, and a woman appeared from the house's interior. She wore tan slacks and a white tunic top. Her gray hair was cropped close on the top and sides, and long in the back.

"Welcome to Gemini." Smiling, the woman extended her hand first to Meg and then to Eric. "I'm Laureen, Carl's house manager."

After greetings were exchanged, Jones said, "Where're we putting 'em?"

"Guest cottages. Miz Evans in Wolf House, Mr. Richards in Bear."

"The cottages are named after Indian clans," Eric commented.

Laureen nodded. "You'll like 'em. They're very comfortable. Here're your keys." She dipped a hand into her tunic pocket and pulled out two key rings, handing one to Meg and the other to Eric. "Oh, and Carl wants you for cocktails before dinner, so be back here by six. And don'tcha be late. Carl's a stickler for bein' on time."

On their way once again, they passed a swimming pool, complete with chaise lounges, umbrella tables, and a cabana. So far, Gemini Island had the appearance of an elegant resort, and Meg idly wondered if as an employee she'd be allowed to take advantage of the amenities.

Jones navigated another bend in the road, and the cart reached the guest cottages, six in all, with three on either side of the road. Miniatures of the main house, they were made from the same stone and wood. In front of each one stood a totem. He pulled to a stop in front of the first cottage. "Miz Evans stays here."

Wolf House, Laureen had called Meg's cottage. Looking up at her totem, Meg saw where the name came from. The carving of a wolf's head topped the pole. Not even the bright sunlight beaming on him could dispel the menacing eyes and razor-edged teeth. She could almost hear him growl and snarl. Was he supposed to scare her? Or protect her? Meg wasn't sure which.

"So where's my place?" Eric looked around.

Meg waited to hear Jones' answer, hoping he would say Eric's cottage was the one farthest away.

Jones thumbed ahead. "Next door."

Darn. Meg pursed her lips. Not only did they have to work together but also live next door to each other. She didn't want him to observe her movements during her free time. If she had other reasons for not wanting him near, she refused to acknowledge what those might be.

Jones took her luggage up to the cottage's loft bedroom.

After he and Eric left, Meg explored her new home. A pine-scented air freshener pervaded the atmosphere. The place was surprisingly spacious, with a bar separating the living and kitchen areas. A hallway led to a bathroom and another small room for storage.

Back in the living room, she paced, wondering what to do now. Her bones ached with fatigue, yet she was too keyed up to take a nap. She glanced at her wristwatch. Nearly four-thirty. Still plenty of time before cocktails and dinner with her new boss.

A walk might help to work off her nervous energy, and also familiarize her with the surroundings. She opened the door to the cottage and stepped out into the sunshine.

****

Clutching a small metal box, Eric paced his

cottage, extending his hand in front. As he approached the phone on the counter between the kitchen and living room, he saw one of the lights on the device blink. Yep, his good ol' bug buster picked 'em up every time. He set down the box, unscrewed the phone's speaker, and studied the insides. Pretty sophisticated. Carl Miller—or whoever installed the bug—was up on the latest technology. Leaving the bug in place, he put the speaker back together.

His search turned up two more such devices. One was buried behind a seascape hanging on the living room wall, and the other was in the loft bedroom behind a painting of Indian dancers.

He left all of the bugs intact. He wouldn't give himself away by tampering with them. Maybe later, if absolutely necessary, he would disarm them. For now, let whoever was responsible listen in.

Time to make a phone call, and the sooner the better. He returned the bug sweeper to the cache under the false bottom of his duffel bag. Pulling his cell phone from his belt clip, he stepped outside the cottage. Making sure no one was around, he tramped the length of the building, through a patch of dark green salal and into a clearing.

The cell phone icon indicated a strong signal. Good. Now if he could reach his party. He punched in the number.

After a few rings, the other party picked up. "Nick here."

"Hey, Nick. It's Eric.

Nick Hinton was a former FBI agent Eric met in training at Quantico. Nick had lasted only a couple years with the Bureau before he quit to become a private investigator. He and Eric often did favors for each other. He hoped Nick could help him with this one. "Can you run a check on someone for me?" He planned to do his own search on the Internet, but Nick would have sources not available there.

"Sure. What ya got?"

Eric scanned the nearby woods for signs someone might be nearby. Except for the soft breeze sighing through the trees, all was quiet. "Her name is Megan Evans."

Nick laughed. "This personal or business?"

"You know me too well, my friend. But this is strictly business. Look for any connection to Fortune Industries."

"You got it. Back at you asap."

"Thanks, Nick. By the way, how's Angie?" Nick's wife was expecting their first child any day now.

Nick's voice dropped a notch. "Miserable. We'll both be glad when junior decides to make an appearance."

"I bet. Give her my best, and let me know when junior arrives, okay?"

They ended the call, and Eric tucked away his phone. He wondered what life would be like with a wife and a child. He'd been married once, shortly after graduation from high school. What a disaster. They both were way too young and self-centered to make a marriage work. Thankfully, they'd had no children, and, once the dust settled, the divorce had been amicable enough. Since then, he avoided a serious commitment. He liked his life free and uncluttered.

He returned to his cottage. A little over an hour remained until he had to be at the main house, plenty of time to start an Internet search. He opened his canvas bag and took out his laptop.

****

When Meg returned to Wolf House, late afternoon sun slanted through the pine trees, bathing her cottage in a glow like something out of a fairy tale. Her stroll had been pleasant, if uneventful. She took a route leading to the beach, a quiet shore far removed from the docks, where calm waters lapped gently onto kelp-strewn sand. Spotting a bench, she sat and rested a while.

Now, she must get ready for dinner with Carl Miller. She climbed the stairs to her loft, wishing she'd asked Laureen if they dressed for dinner. Deciding on a middle ground, she changed from her jeans and T-shirt to slacks, a cotton blouse, and a linen blazer. After untying her ponytail, she shook her head and let her wavy hair cascade over her shoulders. She touched up her lipstick and added a little blusher. Picking up an eyeliner stick, she bent over the sink to better outline her eyes. Then she tossed down the liner and stepped back. Whom was she trying to impress?

Eric Richard's image popped into her mind.

No way. Don't be silly. She wasn't here to flirt or to put on makeup for any man. Especially not for Mr. Richards.

As she stepped out the front door, she couldn't help glancing at Eric's cottage. Should she stop in for him? No, they were only colleagues. Let him find his own way.

At the house, Laureen led Meg to a patio off the dining room. Underneath the transparent roof sat a cart with liquor bottles, an ice bucket, and glasses. Potted plants and boxes of geraniums and dahlias lined the edge of the stone flooring. The smell of wet earth and flowers hung in the air, as though the plants had recently been watered. A coiled hose nearby and several puddles of water on the stones offered confirmation.

Laureen disappeared back inside the house, leaving Meg alone. Meg stood in the shade shifting from one foot to the other, uncertain what to do until her host arrived.

Movement in a dark corner caught her eye. No sound, just shadows moving. A chill washed over her skin. "Is someone there?" Hesitant to explore, she stood her ground.

A man emerged from the shadows and strode toward her. Although his hair was white, his tanned, youthful face put him in his mid-forties. He looked fit and trim in brown slacks and a tan sports shirt with a bolo tie.

"Ms. Evans?"

"Yes, and you're Mr. Miller?"

"Please call me Carl." He extended his hand.

Meg relaxed as she shook his hand. "And you can call me Meg."

"Have a seat." Carl gestured toward several rattan chairs near the liquor cart. "Eric Richards will be joining us.

Meg sat, feeling her stomach clench at the mention of the troublesome man. "Yes, I met him at the Orcas ferry dock. I was surprised to learn someone else would be working on your collection."

Carl settled in a chair across from her. "Eric and I met only recently, after Kent Gheller hired you. I thought Eric would be good to have aboard. He shares my passion for Northwest Indian art." He raised an eyebrow. "I hope working together won't be a problem."

"No, of course not."

"I'm glad to hear that. After dinner, I'll give you both a tour of the museum." He gestured toward the liquor cart. "What would you like to drink?"

"A glass of white wine would be nice."

"Of course." He snapped his fingers. "Burke!"

A man stepped from the bushes surrounding the patio.

Meg gave a start and bit back a gasp. She had no idea anyone else was nearby. Did everyone here make a habit of hiding in the shadows? Knowing a stranger had been listening in on their conversation, however innocent, gave her the creeps.

Like Jones, Burke had a wrestler's build, but he was even larger and more muscular than his counterpart. Spikes of bleached blond hair sprouted from the top of his head, and a snake tattoo decorated one bare arm. A gold earring in his left earlobe caught the sunlight.

Carl introduced them, adding, "A glass of the Chardonnay for Meg, and I'll have my usual."

Burke nodded and busied himself pouring their drinks.

Carl's usual turned out to be a blended whiskey with a splash of soda. Burke delivered the drinks, hardly glancing at Meg as he handed her the wine. His duty done, he faded back into the shadows.

Carl sipped his drink. "While we're waiting for Eric, tell me about yourself."

His question puzzled Meg. Wasn't everything he needed to know on her resume? But, since Kent Gheller had hired her, perhaps Carl hadn't seen her resume. Or, perhaps he was only making polite conversation. "What would you like to know?"

"The usual." He made a dismissive wave. "Do you have family?"

"I'm divorced."

"Children?"

Alyssa's beautiful features flashed across her mind, and Meg gripped her wineglass. "Ah...one." She rushed on. "And, I've had experience working in a museum."

"The Seattle Art Museum, as I recall."

So he had seen her resume. "That's right, I helped to catalog a collection of lithographs. I don't know too much about Northwest Indian art, but I've been reading up on the subject." She raised her free hand in mock protest. "But I hope you won't put me to the test."

He laughed. "Don't worry about authenticating anything. That's Eric's job. And, even though I've moved up the date of the museum's opening, I'm no slave driver. You'll have time to rest and relax while you're here."

"I'm looking forward to exploring the island. Especially your mountain." She turned to glance at the peak, now a black silhouette against the pale sky, and then glanced at Carl in time to see a frown crease his brow.

"Unfortunately, that side of the island, including Mt. Gemini, is closed to guests.

"Oh?" She raised her eyebrows. Interesting situation.

"Yes, the area is undeveloped and wild. Until we clear away the underbrush and pave trails, I want everyone to keep out. A liability issue. You understand."

His tone seemed unnecessarily hard. Was there some other reason behind his warning? "Of course, but I must admit I'm disappointed."

"You'll find plenty of other things to do. I expect to see you around the pool during your time off."

At that moment, Eric strode onto the patio.

Carl stood and extended his hand. "Ah, Eric. Good to see you again."

"Great to be here." Eric shook Carl's hand.

Eric's navy slacks and blue cotton shirt suggested he'd given some thought to dressing for dinner. His hair glistened with moisture, as though he'd recently showered.

An image of him naked under hot, streaming water popped into Meg's mind. He would be all tight muscle, not an ounce of fat anywhere. Warmth pooled in the pit of her stomach. The blatantly sexual response surprised—and disturbed—her. Hadn't she already decided she didn't like the man?

Grinning, Eric turned to her. "Ah, my assistant is already here."

Assistant. Meg ground her teeth. If Mr. Eric Richards planned on being her boss, he was in for a rude awakening.

Chapter Four

Half an hour later, Laureen summoned them inside to dinner.

Although she'd kept up her end of the conversation, Meg was relieved to have the cocktail hour's small talk over. Her uncertainties about both men kept her nerves on edge. Dinner promised a welcome distraction.

In the dining room, Indian ceremonial masks hung on walls covered with a woven brown fabric. Other decorations included paintings of Northwest landscapes and a few abstract prints in colors matching the red, black, and blue masks.

Carl directed them to their seats at a rectangular table covered in white linen.

A man in his twenties joined them. His brown hair resembled a bird's nest, and his rumpled khakis and denim shirt looked as though they'd been slept in.

"Sorry to be late, Carl. I was in the middle of something."

Carl pursed his lips and shook his head. "You're always in the middle of something. Sit and relax." He motioned to the remaining place setting at the table. "This is Lester Wakowski. He's our resident computer expert."

Lester slipped into the seat, and then gazed at Meg and Eric through his black-framed eyeglasses. "Glad to meetcha."

Laureen served grilled salmon, rice pilaf, and sautéed asparagus, all of which looked and smelled wonderful, and Burke filled their wineglasses from a chilled bottle of Pinot Noir. Carl's lifestyle quite surpassed Meg's, even after she and Johnny had moved to Forest Glen. Too bad she had come here for such a dark purpose. Otherwise, she could pretend this was a glamorous vacation.

Carl and Eric discussed their mutual interest in Northwest Indian art.

Far from being an expert, Meg chose to avoid their conversation. She looked across the table at Lester, who also had stayed out of the other men's discussion. "How do you like Gemini Island, Lester?"

Lester pushed up his glasses with his forefinger. "It's okay, but I like the city better."

"You mean Seattle?"

"Nah, the Bellevue-Redmond area. That's where the action is. My kinda action. You know, Microsoft, TechSmart, CompAct."

"Right, Carl said you're his computer expert." Intent on keeping the conversation going, Meg offered an encouraging smile.

Lester straightened and stuck out his chest. "Yep. For the past week, I've been setting up Carl's system, including the one you'll use for cataloging. But, hey, this is just baby stuff. I'm working on something a whole lot bigger."

"Really?" Meg kept her gaze on him while helping herself to another sourdough roll from the breadbasket.

"Uh huh, but don't ask me about it. No can tell. Just need to fine tune it and then get my man here"—he nodded toward Carl—"to fork over the dough for the start-up."

"I see. And he said he would?" Meg darted a look at Carl. He was still talking to Eric, waving a hand for emphasis.

"No problemo. Carl's real good about helping his employees strike out on their own. That's how Fortune Industries started. A benefactor came along and gave him a leg up, and now he's passing it forward."

Thinking now was a good time to start her inquiry, she leaned forward and said in a low tone, "A friend of a friend used to work for Fortune."

Lester snorted. "Everybody knows somebody who works there. It's a big place."

"He was an accountant—"

Carl swiveled in her direction. "What did you say, Meg? You know someone who works for me?"

Eric, too, turned to look at Meg, eyebrow raised. "What's the person's name?"

Meg tightened her grip on her fork. "I, ah, a friend of a friend."

Carl nodded. "Okay, what is the person's name? Oh, come on, quiz me. I pride myself in knowing my employees' names."

Meg's heartbeat raced. "I'm not sure, but I think his name is"—she gazed at the ceiling—"Jerome. Yes, Jerome something." She held her breath, hoping he would buy her story, hoping he hadn't heard the "accountant" part of her query to Lester.

Carl closed his eyes and tapped his fingers on the table. His onyx ring sparkled under the light. Finally, he opened his eyes, frowned, and shook his head. "You've got me. Don't know any Jeromes."

She exhaled and shrugged. "It's not important."

Eric raised both eyebrows.

He doesn't believe me. Clenching her napkin, she groped for something to say if he questioned her further.

"Ta da." Laureen entered the room carrying a silver tray loaded with individual servings of sponge cake, each piled high with fresh strawberries and swirls of whipped cream.

"Ah, dessert." Carl rubbed his hands together.

Laureen set the tray on the sideboard and picked up two of the plates. "Berries from our own garden and cake baked fresh today." She set one of the desserts in front of Meg and the other at Eric's place.

Meg wanted to say, "Good timing, Laureen." Instead, she said, "This looks delicious." And it was. The cake was moist and flavorful and the berries sweet and ripe. Conversation ceased as everyone dug in and enjoyed the treat.

Lester wolfed down his cake, and then scooted back his chair and stood. "Excuse, please. Gotta work on my project." He turned to their host. "Okay, Carl?"

Without looking up from chasing the last strawberry around his plate, Carl made a dismissive wave. "Go, already."

****

"Want to walk or take a cart?" Carl asked after dinner was over, and Meg joined him and Eric outside for the promised tour of the museum.

Meg breathed in the soft evening air. "A walk might be pleasant."

Eric nodded. "A walk'll give me a chance to stretch my legs."

They started off, Carl leading them along one of the island's many paths. Soon they left the house behind and entered the woods. Dusk spread a soft pink glow above the trees. The air smelled of earth and leaves and the occasional sweetness of wild flowers.

Carl's museum was as impressive as his house. The structure was entirely of cedar, he told them, the traditional wood used for Northwest Indian longhouses. Carvings of various Indian emblems—wolf, raven, bear, and whale—decorated a triangle above the double doors.

"We're still developing the area." Carl nodded toward a mini-tractor and a backhoe parked nearby. "This will be a garden and a patio where guests can relax and have refreshments."

He unlocked the double doors and they went inside.

A rush of cedar fragrance flooded Meg's nostrils, reminding her of a cedar trinket box she had at home. Sometimes, she would open it only to inhale the fragrant aroma.

Carl flipped several light switches and overhead fluorescents beamed to life.

They passed through an entry then into a room where empty glass display cases lined the walls.

Carl pointed to a canoe suspended by wires from the two-story ceiling. "What do you think of this? Fifty feet long and carved from one cedar log. Takes ten oarsmen and can carry five tons.

Meg hid a smile. Carl sounded like a proud father discussing his offspring.

Eric gave a low whistle. "Impressive."

"Of course, you recognize the killer whale carvings

on the sides?" Carl aimed his question at Eric.

Meg was glad he hadn't asked her. Despite the research she'd done, she wasn't sure she could give the correct answer.

Eric narrowed his eyes and tipped his head from one side to the other. Finally, he said, "Tlingit."

Carl shook his head. "No, actually, the Haida made it. But it could have been used by the Tlingit, because they bought many of their canoes from the Haida."

"Sure. I was about to add that."

Something about Eric's tone didn't ring true. Meg wanted to catch his eye, but he avoided her, focusing on the canoe, as though fascinated.

Carl pointed to a doorway across the room. "Come on, I'll show you where you'll be working."

Meg and Eric fell into step behind him. He led them down a dim hallway to a room where tables were stacked with Indian artifacts—masks, bowls, boxes, hats, and paintings. Other furnishings included a filing cabinet and two desks—one piled with books, the other with a computer and printer.

"That's your station, Meg." Carl indicated the desk with the computer. "The software program for your cataloging is already installed. Check it out why don't you, while Eric and I look at the stuff on the tables."

She switched on the computer and studied the program long enough to decide using it would be simple enough. Then she shut off the machine and went to join the men. They were discussing a conical hat made of reeds, which Eric held. Meg let her gaze glide over Eric's broad back, shoulders, and strong arms, the muscles cording as he turned the hat over in his hands.

She wondered what kind of lover he would be. No

doubt, a good one. Heat crept up her neck and onto her face.

Carl turned. "What do you think of the program?"

Meg pressed a hand to her cheek, hoping to cover her blush. "I'm sure I'll manage it with no problem."

"I hope so." Eric eyed her. "Because I'll be plenty busy with my job." He made a sweeping gesture at the tables.

Meg dropped her hand and lifted her chin. "Don't worry, you won't have to baby-sit me."

"Is there a problem here?" Carl's gaze slid from Eric to Meg. "Something I'm not in on?"

"No, nothing." Meg pasted on a smile.

Keeping his gaze on Meg, Eric nodded. "We'll do just fine."

On the way back to the main house, Carl told them he was leaving the following day for a trip to Seattle. "I'll be back in a couple days," he added. "And on Friday, guests will arrive for the weekend. Be ready to take a break so that you can join in the fun."

At the house, Carl herded them into his office to peruse the museum's architectural plans, which were spread out on a work table.

Although Meg was interested, she finally gave in to a yawn. She turned away, but not fast enough to escape Eric's notice.

"Are we boring you?" he drawled.

Meg clamped her jaw shut. "Not at all. It's been a long day. I was up at five to catch the bus for Anacortes."

Carl looked at his wristwatch. "The time is getting late. But how about a drink before you turn in?"

"No, thank you," Meg said.

Eric hesitated but then shook his head. "Thanks, Carl, but I'll pass, too. I'll walk Meg back to her cottage."

"You don't need to go with me. I can find my way." Sarcasm laced her voice, but she was too tired to care.

"I've no doubt you can," Eric said, "but I'm ready to call it a night, too. We might as well walk back together.

Carl rolled up the plans and slid them back into their cardboard tube. "I'll see you both in a couple days. Any problems with your work, ask Lester. Anything else, Laureen should be able to handle. And, like I said, be ready to party this weekend."

****

Outside, the globe lights illuminated the walkway to the cottages. A rising half moon hovered above the trees, and a light breeze carried the damp smell of the water. Meg walked beside Eric in silence, the tension between them palpable.

Then he stopped and held out his hand. "Look, being nasty won't do either of us any good. How 'bout a truce?"

She stared at the well-shaped fingers she'd admired while in the museum, and then looked into his eyes. They were heavily shadowed in the fading light, but she detected sincerity in their depths, and in his voice, as well. "All right." She clasped his hand.

He curled his fingers around hers in a warm, firm grip. "There, that's better. Isn't it?"

"If you say so.

"I do say so. Come on, we'll get you to your cottage." He motioned them forward.

"Yes, I am tired." Stifling another yawn, she fell into step beside him.

"Sure is dark without city lights, isn't it?"

She had to smile at his effort to be nice. Cooperating wouldn't hurt. She gazed up at the sky. "It is dark."

"You live in Seattle?"

"Uh huh."

"In the 'burbs?"

"No, on Queen Anne Hill."

He held aside a pine branch hanging over the path. "Ah, a city woman. Bet you have a great view of the Space Needle."

"I do." Despite her annoyance with the man, she found herself warming to the conversation. "Seattle Center is one of my favorite places. What about you? Where do you live?"

"Apartment in the University District. You have family in the city?"

Uh oh, dangerous territory. Meg's shoulders tensed. Yet, withdrawing now might only pique his curiosity. "I'm divorced. My parents passed away a few years ago."

"I'm divorced, too. No children, and no other family in the area."

Meg let pass the opportunity to mention she was a parent. Then guilt gripped her and her breath hitched in her throat. To not mention Aly was tantamount to denying she ever existed. Still, to tell Eric about her daughter's tragic death might invite more inquiry. Answering personal questions would reveal more than she wanted anyone here to know.

Fortunately, they rounded a corner and her cottage

came into view. Meg's inward sigh of relief was short-lived. The landscape light shining on the wolf totem gave his long, sharp teeth and curled tongue a menacing look. She shivered and hugged her arms.

"Cold?"

"No. The wolf totem gave me a start. With the light shining on him, he looks…evil."

Eric gazed at the totem. "He does." Then he focused on her again. "He's a good guard, though, don't you think?"

She arched an eyebrow. "Do I need guarding?"

"One never knows. You can't be too careful, especially in strange places."

****

Inside her cottage, Meg leaned against the front door and listened to Eric's footsteps fade. Their so-called truce hadn't done much to ease her nervousness. Working with him in the confines of the museum promised to be a challenge.

She flipped on the overhead light and crossed the room. Midway, she stopped in her tracks. Her sixth sense told her someone had been there during her absence. Her heart thudded. She sucked in her breath and looked around for something amiss to support her suspicion.

The water glass she'd left on the kitchen counter was still there, as were the reference books and notepad left on the coffee table. Nothing appeared to have been disturbed.

She gazed up at the loft. Maybe she'd find evidence there. She headed toward the stairs and then stopped. What if an intruder was up there, hiding in the shadows?

No, she was sure she was alone. Someone had been here but now was gone. Still, her heart hammered as she placed her foot on the first step.

At the top, she groped the wall and found the light switch. The room sprang to life. Her heart still pounding, she gazed around. A pair of black shoes she'd left near the closet door now lay in the center of the room. She gasped. Her hunch was correct. Someone *had* been there.

She crossed to the closet. Holding her breath, half expecting someone to jump out, she flung open the folding doors. All her clothing, which she had hung evenly spaced out, had been pushed to one end. More evidence of an intruder.

In the bathroom, her cosmetic case, which she'd zipped closed after refreshing her makeup, gaped open on the marble counter. A stray lipstick lay nearby. She found her hairbrush on the floor. Feeling violated, she snatched up the brush and clutched it to her chest.

Her first impulse was to call Carl Miller. She went to the bedside phone, reached for the receiver, and then let her hand drop. She would not call him. Nothing had been taken, and she wanted to keep a low profile, so that when she had the chance, she could investigate the island.

She strode to the window, parted the slats, and peered out. All was dark, except for a single light twinkling through the trees in the direction of Eric's cottage. No, she wouldn't run to him, either. He would think she was a silly, hysterical woman, one more reason why she wasn't qualified to be his "assistant."

Her mind whirling with questions, she turned from the window and prepared for bed. Who would search her belongings? A petty thief? Or someone who knew her true identity and her relationship to Johnny? If Johnny's accident had been deliberately caused, that meant he'd been a threat to someone. Did they now find her a threat, as well?

****

Eric sat on his sofa, reading Nick's message on his cell phone. His buddy had discovered some very interesting information about Megan Evans—and her ex-husband, Johnny Stanton.

Johnny's death had been ruled an accident. But was it, really? Or was foul play involved? Was Meg here for the same reason he was? If so, she was a complication he didn't want. Since he couldn't be sure, he wouldn't take her into his confidence and instead would work alone. He'd have to make sure she didn't interfere with his investigation.

He turned out the downstairs lights and climbed the stairs to the loft. In the bathroom, he reached to unzip his leather bag and retrieve his toothbrush, only to find the bag already open. He'd used some of the items to freshen up for dinner, but he was certain when he finished he'd replaced them and zipped up the bag. He sorted through the contents. As far as he could tell, everything was there. Nothing else in the bathroom appeared out of place.

In the bedroom, his canvas bag sat near the closet where he'd left it. Yep, the bag also had been pawed through. But, again, nothing was missing. Underneath the false bottom, his bug sweeper, Glock .22, night-vision binoculars, infrared camera, and a few other items he didn't want discovered, were undisturbed.

Eric paced, rubbing the back of his neck. What was

going on? Maybe Carl sent one of his goons to snoop on all his guests. Or, maybe the person acted on his own.

Worse yet, maybe someone had figured out why he was really here. If so, he'd better be extra careful.

No matter what the reason for the search, he would not be deterred from his purpose. He made a fist and pounded his palm. Nothing would keep him from finding out what had happened to Norrie.

****

Meg sits next to Johnny in the front seat of his SUV. Alyssa is asleep in the back seat. They're driving through the darkness and the rain. Johnny steps on the gas and the car races forward.

"You're driving too fast!" she yells. "You're drunk!"

He turns, his handsome features twisted into a sneer.

A bolt of lightning illuminates the road ahead. The pavement is as shiny as a new nickel.

"There's a curve! Slow down!"

Thunder rolls across the sky, and Johnny hits the brakes. But it's too late. The SUV skids and crashes through the guardrail. Meg screams as they sail over the cliff.

A shout echoes into the night.

Gasping for breath, Meg bolted upright in the bed. The nightmare again—the one about Johnny and Alyssa's accident. The awful dream had plagued her since that fateful night. Of course, she had not been in the car with Johnny and Alyssa when it went over the cliff. But in the dream, she always was with them.

Tonight's dream was different. The shout at the

end sounded real, as though it came not from her dream but from outside her cottage. Meg tilted her head and listened. Two more shouts rang out, the second lower in timbre than the first. Two people?

The disruption came from behind her cottage. She climbed from bed and crept to the window. Parting the blinds, she peered out. Beyond the patio and a small patch of grass lay thick, dark woods. She unlatched and pushed open the window. Cool, damp air rushed in, along with the sound of rustling in the underbrush.

Without stopping to consider the possible consequences, she shut the window and grabbed her jeans. She tugged them on, pulled a sweatshirt over her head, and stuffed her feet into her tennis shoes. Digging into her suitcase, she found the miniature flashlight she'd brought and slipped it into her pocket.

She ran down the stairs and along the hallway to the back door. Once outside, she paused to get her bearings. Moonlight outlined two wooden Adirondack chairs and several flower boxes on the patio. Beyond lay a patch of the grass with a dirt path leading into the woods. Taking a deep breath, she headed toward the path.

****

Eric rolled over in bed and punched up his pillow. Sleep tonight had been intermittent. Too many things on his mind, plus an unfamiliar bed. He'd just laid down his head again when shouting outside broke the silence. He couldn't make out the words, but judging by the noise, two people were having a helluva fight.

Jumping out of bed, he hurried to the window overlooking the back yard. The blast of cool air when he opened the window jolted him fully awake. The shouting was louder now and definitely coming from the woods in back of the cottage.

He snatched his jeans from a chair and stuck in one leg and then the other. Pulled on his T-shirt. Planted his feet into his shoes and laced them up. Opening his duffel, he pulled up the false bottom and grabbed his gun. Snapping the weapon to the inside of his belt took only a couple seconds. He grabbed his jacket from where he'd tossed it onto a chair and shrugged into it. Okay, ready for whatever.

He crept downstairs and out the back door. He knew the lay of the land from when he'd come out earlier to make his phone call to Nick. Stone patio with a few pieces of furniture, grass, and then a path leading into thick woods. A quick glance around revealed nothing had changed. The forest was where he needed to be. He started off.

The path into the trees was a narrow dirt track, one of the many he'd already encountered in the short time he'd been on Gemini. The island was a veritable labyrinth. He had no idea where he was going, except that the general direction was toward the water. Yeah, right. Brilliant deduction.

The shouting had stopped, but rustling in the underbrush up ahead indicated someone—or something—was still there. He forged on, pushing aside branches, dodging dips in the path, twisting and turning, plunging deeper and deeper into the forest.

He reached a small clearing filled with rocks, some the size of boulders, and salal and sword fern. On the other side, where the woods began again, two figures bobbed along. All he could see above the underbrush were their heads and shoulders.

He couldn't tell whether they were male or female. Just two people. He didn't think they were Jones and Burke. Burke had spiky hair, and both of these heads appeared round on top. Besides, their shoulders weren't as broad and thick as those on Carl's goons.

In case the two looked around in his direction, Eric skirted the edge of the clearing before taking up their tail again. He'd barely reached the path they were on when someone leaped from the bushes in front of him.

Chapter Five

With no time to dodge the guy, Eric ran smack into the body. He gave a little yelp and whirled around. Moonlight shone down on wide, startled eyes and an open mouth.

The guy was a woman.

Meg Evans.

What was she doing here? He glanced from her to the two figures ahead. They'd stopped and were looking around. Eric grabbed Meg by the waist then pulled her off the path and into the bushes.

She squirmed and struggled.

He clamped his hand over her mouth and whispered, "Quiet.

Not trusting she wouldn't cry out again, he kept her mouth covered. Her breasts under her sweatshirt were soft and her hair smelled of roses.

After a minute more of silence, he dared to raise his head. The two figures were continuing down the path. He waited until they were out of sight and then put his mouth close to Meg's ear. "They're gone. But stay still."

She nodded.

He pulled his hand away from her mouth.

Shaking her head, she sat up and glared, and then swiped her lips with the back of her hand.

He glared back. "What the hell are you doing

here?"

"What are *you* doing here?"

Careful. He didn't want to give away too much. "I heard someone shouting. I came to find out what was going on."

She tugged a twig from her hair and tossed it away. "Me, too."

"Did you stop to think that might be dangerous? Apparently not."

"So it's okay for you to be here, but not for me? What kind of sense does that make?"

"None to you, I guess. But I'm a guy. Guys take risks."

"And women don't?" She huffed. "I thought someone might be hurt and need help."

Frustration filled him, and he threw up his hands. "Okay, okay, no more arguing. They're gone now. We might as well go back to our cottages." He stood and held out his hand.

Ignoring his offer, she grabbed onto a bush and struggled to her feet.

He placed his hand on her arm. "Are you okay?"

She shook him off and brushed the dirt and twigs from her sweatshirt. "Yes, but no thanks to you."

"Sorry, but I didn't want whoever it was to see us. I don't know what was going on."

"I don't know, either. And you were probably right to keep us quiet.

Her grudging tone grated, and he didn't bother to hide his sarcasm. "Thanks for the vote of confidence." What he wanted to say was, "Thanks for nothing." She had ruined his chances of maybe discovering something important.

Eric leading the way, they headed back to their cottages, twisting and turning along the narrow path. "Any idea who those two were?" he asked over his shoulder.

She stepped aside to dodge a protruding tree branch. "Not a clue. They weren't big enough to be Burke or Jones."

"That's what I thought. Carl and Lester, maybe? Or people we haven't met yet?"

"Maybe. But does it matter?"

He shrugged. "Not a bit. Nope. None of our business."

"You're right. None of our business."

****

Several hours later, when Meg's alarm clock jolted her awake, she groped for the Snooze button. After first her nightmare and then her trip into the woods, extra sleep would be nice. Then she remembered today was her first day on the job. Even though she knew Carl Miller had gone to Seattle, she had no doubt word would reach him if she didn't report to work on time. With a sigh, she tossed back the covers, stood, and headed for the bathroom.

Later, trudging along the path to the main house, eager for breakfast, she thought about last night's incident. She told Eric she went into the woods to see if anyone needed help. Which was true. In part. Had he believed her?

But what about his reason for investigating the noises? Just a 'guy thing,' as he would have her believe?

When he pulled her into the bushes and whispered in her ear, something hard attached to his hip pressed into her side. She looked to see what it was, but his jacket covered the object. Had he been wearing a gun? But why would he arm himself to investigate a noise on the island, unless he expected to find danger?

A chill skittered down her spine, and she hugged her arms. Who was he, really? A software consultant and an authority on Northwest Indian artifacts? Or someone else?

At the main house, she entered by the back door and headed for the dining room. No one was there, but the sideboard held chafing dishes of eggs and bacon, baskets of toast and muffins, and bowls of fresh fruit. Carl really went all out to feed his guests. Meg eagerly eyed the food, but first, a cup of much-needed coffee. She poured herself a mugful from a silver urn and wandered to the sliding glass doors. Outside on the patio, Jones, with his black ponytail curled over his shoulder, watered the geraniums and dahlias in the redwood boxes. He didn't look up.

Laureen bustled in carrying a tray loaded with jars of jam. Her tan slacks and white tunic top looked crisp and clean, and her hair appeared freshly gelled on top. "Good morning," she chirped. "Sleep well?"

Ah, the perfect opportunity to find out about last night. Presuming Laureen knew—and was willing to tell. Meg had already decided to keep quiet about a possible cottage intruder, but discussing the trouble in the woods would be safe enough. She claimed a place at the table with her mug and then went to the sideboard to fill a plate. "I slept okay at first, but then noise outside woke me. It sounded like people shouting."

Laureen frowned and unloaded the jams next to the basket of toast and muffins. "I didn't hear anything around here. I slept like a baby."

"The commotion came from the woods behind my cottage." Meg spooned scrambled eggs onto her plate. "I looked out the window and thought I saw two people." Just a little stretch of the truth.

"I'll ask Jones if he knows anything." Leaving the tray on the sideboard, she opened the sliding glass doors and called, "Jonesy! Come here a sec!"

Jones looked up from his watering, his gaze moving from Laureen to Meg. He frowned, but he tossed down the hose and ambled over to turn off the faucet. "Whatcha want?" he said when he met them at the open door.

"Don't come in." Laureen pointed to his leather boots, glistening with water and sludge. "Meg here wants to know about something she saw last night."

Jones' narrow-eyed gaze focused on Meg. "So whaddya want to know?"

She went over her story, careful to keep the same details she'd told Laureen.

He nodded. "Coupla kids. Nothin' to worry about. Me 'n Burke run 'em off."

"Kids? From nearby islands?" Meg looked from him to Laureen.

"Yep. They come here to party," Laureen explained. "But don't worry, Jonesy and Burke take care of them. Nothin' much gets by them. Huh, Jonesy?"

"Right." Jones fisted his hands and boxed the air. Then he turned away and went back to his watering.

Laureen closed the door and smiled. "Yep, our guys are good watchdogs. You don't have to worry about being safe here. Trust me."

****

An hour later, Meg pulled open the museum's heavy door and stepped inside. She allowed her eyes to adjust to the dim interior, and then picked her way across the cavernous main room, past the empty glass cases, and down the dim hallway to the workroom.

Laureen had said Eric ate breakfast early, so she expected to find him hard at work. But, no, he wasn't at his desk, or at any of the tables stacked with artifacts, or elsewhere in the room. Then she spotted him outside on the patio. His back was to her, and he held a cell phone to his ear. Meg crept toward the open patio door. Not that she wanted to eavesdrop….

"You did good, Nick," Eric was saying. "I owe you one… No, I hope she won't be here much longer. We'll see…

Her stomach clenched. Was he talking about her? He must be. How many other "shes" were on the island? And what did he mean, he hoped she wouldn't be here long?

Eric suddenly turned in her direction.

Intending to flatten herself against the wall, Meg jumped sideways. Her foot hit the glass with a dull thud. Before she could recover and hide, she connected with his gaze.

His eyebrows shot up and then lowered into a frown. "Talk to you later," he said into the phone, and with long-legged strides, he headed toward the door.

"Hey." Meg pasted on an innocent smile.

He stepped into the room. "Morning." While slipping his phone into its belt holder, he studied her.

She held her breath, waiting to see if he would boldly ask if she were eavesdropping. "Didn't see you when I came in and wondered where you were," she finally said.

"I had business to take care of. Ready to go to work?"

"Yes, I am." The crisis apparently over, Meg eyed her desk, where the computer waited.

He crossed to his workbench and shuffled through a stack of index cards. "Did you get any sleep last night after our little adventure?"

Meg went to her desk, sat, and switched on the computer. "Enough. Oh, I told Laureen what happened. I changed the story a little, though. I didn't say I went outside or that I ran into you. I just said I heard the shouts and saw two people from my window."

He looked over his shoulder and raised an eyebrow. "Oh? And what did she say?"

"She asked Jones, and he said they were a couple of kids. He and Burke ran them off."

"Kids?" He put down the cards and gave her his full attention.

"Uh huh. Laureen said kids come here from the other islands sometimes to party. But what do you think?"

He shrugged. "I'm satisfied. How about you?"

"I guess.

"Good. We'll get busy. I've put aside a few items you can start on. C'mon over here." He motioned to his workbench.

Meg went to stand beside him. Today he wore jeans and a light tan shirt with the sleeves rolled up to the elbows. The light from nearby windows caught the fine hairs on his bare arms and played along corded muscles as he picked up one object and then another.

She hardly noticed what the artifacts were. Instead, she visualized his strong arms gripping her yesterday as he lifted her into the boat, and again last night when he pulled her into the bushes. Heat filled her, and she took a step back. Like that would do any good.

"…Notes you can record, too.

She jolted to attention. "What?"

He frowned. "Notes. There." He pointed to a stack of three-by-five index cards.

"Oh, right."

"Be sure to get the notes matched with the proper item. Give each item a number."

Meg pursed her lips. "I know. Carl went over the instructions last night.

"Yeah, well, you were looking a little out of it just now."

"I'm not out of it. I know my job." She scooped up the cards, strode to her desk, and sat.

Eric stayed on his side of the room.

Now she'd put distance between them, she breathed easier. She studied the first card, which detailed a Haida club made of whalebone, and entered the data in the computer program.

Still, as she'd feared, his presence kept her nerves humming. She wished she were working alone. That he was annoying was enough of a distraction. He had no right to be attractive as well. After a while, she risked a glance over her shoulder.

He was examining a red-and-black facemask. Frowning, he turned it over in his hands. Then he put down the mask and rapidly paged through one of Carl's reference books lying open on the bench.

Meg was certain the mask belonged to the Tlingit

tribe. It had one closed eye, and the Tlingit shaman masks often had asymmetrical elements. Wouldn't Eric know that? He was the expert, after all. Should she tell him what she thought? She opened her mouth and then clamped it shut.

Mind your own business.

****

At noon, Laureen arrived with a picnic basket. "You can eat outside," she told Meg and Eric, and then went directly to the patio where she unloaded the food on a glass-top table.

Following her, Meg gazed up at the patches of blue sky visible above the treetops. "It is a beautiful day."

Laureen unwrapped a paper plate filled with sandwiches. "Yeah, but the island can be miserable when it rains. All these trees dripping on you." She gazed overhead.

Eric came out and pulled two wrought iron chairs up to the table. He motioned Meg into one, and then sat in the other. "Do you stay here all the time, Laureen?"

"Just about. Carl likes to come here all year 'round. Someone needs to keep the place going." She added slices of melon and chocolate cake to the sandwiches, and then set a thermos and paper cups on the table.

"This looks great, Laureen." Eric held out the sandwiches to Meg. "Carl gives you days off, though, right?"

Laureen tucked a wisp of hair behind her ear. "He sure does. Jonesy and Burke, too. We stagger them, so we're not all gone at once."

"Join us." Eric waved at an empty chair.

"No, thanks." Laureen backed away. "I'll leave you to it. Got to get back."

Watching Laureen head down the path to the house, Meg wondered why Eric extended the invitation. Why was he interested in knowing all about Carl's employee? Was he just being polite? Or something else?

****

They finished lunch and returned to their workstations. An hour passed, and then Eric put down the carved wooden bowl he was examining and turned to Meg. "I need a break. I'll run the picnic stuff back to the main house. You okay with that?"

"Sure." Meg didn't miss a stroke on her keyboard. "I still have plenty to do. I haven't finished these cards of Carl's yet, and then I'll start on yours."

When she was alone, Meg worked a while longer and then decided she, too, needed a break. She stood, stretched her arms, and rolled her head back and forth to ease the kinks from her neck. Pouring a glass of water from the pitcher Laureen left, she then wandered over to Eric's workbench.

The five note cards he'd filled out today didn't seem like many for the amount of time he'd spent researching. She picked up the mask with the single closed eye he'd examined earlier along with the corresponding card and saw he'd identified the mask as Haida. No way. Even with her limited knowledge, she was certain the Tlingit Indians made the artifact.

Should she call him on his mistake? Or keep quiet and make the correction when she entered the data into the computer? She returned to her desk and her typing, expecting Eric to pop in any minute, but time passed with no sign of him. He'd had plenty of time to complete his errand. What could be keeping him?

Chapter Six

As he'd told Meg, Eric delivered the picnic basket to Laureen. But then, instead of returning directly to the museum, he took the path to the cottages. When he reached Bear House, he tramped around to the back yard, past his patio, and followed the same route into the woods he'd taken the previous night.

What Jones told Meg about kids using the island to party might be true. Or not. Whatever, he intended to check out the area and see if he could find anything of interest. He knew he ran the risk of running into Jones or Burke, but so what? He was taking a lunch break. They couldn't expect him to stay shut inside the museum all the time.

Even though the sun shone, the towering cedar and pine trees all but closed out the sky, and the forest was dark. The air was cooler, too, than out in the open, and carried the scents of pine and fir, and salt water drifting in from the shore.

Eric took his time, studying the ground, pushing back tree and bush branches, looking for something, anything, the kids—or whoever—may have dropped. He reached the place where he and Meg bumped into each other. The bushes where they'd hidden were mashed and broken. He recalled her body under his, soft and warm.

Cut it out, man. She's trouble.

He continued on until he came to the spot where he last saw the two strangers. Not a sign they—or anyone—had been there. He pushed on, even though a glance at his wristwatch told him he'd been gone over an hour. Meg would be wondering where he was. Just a little farther, and he'd give up.

He reached several forks in the path. One headed toward the mountain, one to the beach, and the other, back to the main house. Maybe. The island had more paths than New York's Central Park, and unless you knew them well, you could waste a lot of time reaching your destination. Okay, he'd gone far enough for today. His search was a waste of time.

Then, as he wheeled around to retrace his steps, he spotted a folded scrap of paper on the ground, half hidden by a low branch of a skinny pine tree. With thumb and forefinger, he carefully plucked the paper from its resting place. He carried it several yards ahead to a sunlit space and carefully unfolded it.

Not one, but four pieces of paper, each about three inches by four inches, all stained and dirty, and with deep creases, as though they had been folded and unfolded many times.

The top piece had long, straight lines intersected at intervals by shorter lines. Faint letters along one line spelled out L-A-S-V-E-G-A-S and then B-L-V-D. Okay, Las Vegas Boulevard. So, this was a map of a small part of Las Vegas' well-known thoroughfare.

The other papers appeared to be map fragments, too. He'd study them later. Right now, he'd better get out of here before someone came along. He refolded the papers along the well-worn creases and stuck them in his jeans' pocket.

****

Dinner that evening, with only Eric and Lester as company, proved awkward for Meg. Eric focused on Lester, engaging him in the same probing he'd done with Laureen.

Lester was only too willing to talk about himself. To a point. His special project was still off limits. "No, no, no." Lester shook his head. "I'm not telling you anymore."

Eric sat back and folded his arms. "I thought you might be interested in some sources of venture capital."

"Nah, I'm set."

Eric quirked an eyebrow. "Carl?"

"Okay, I guess it doesn't hurt to let that out." Lester made a dismissive wave.

Their conversation continued, and soon Meg grew bored and restless. While the two men were still talking, she finished her coffee, made an excuse the two acknowledged with only nods, and left.

Back at her cottage, she kicked off her shoes and then settled on the sofa with one of the reference books she'd brought along. She opened it and read a page but couldn't concentrate. After being left out of the conversation at dinner, she craved someone to talk to. But who?

She finally phoned Davina Ambrose, who had been her next-door neighbor at Forest Glen, where Meg had lived when she'd been married to Johnny. Davina became a good friend, and Meg helped her to establish a home-based business selling her jewelry creations.

"Good to hear from you, Meg," Davina said when she answered Meg's call.

"Good to hear your voice, too. I missed seeing you

the last time I was at the house."

Davina filled in Meg on her jewelry business, and then Meg told Davina about her job on Gemini. "I needed to get away for a while," she said.

"I understand. I've heard of Gemini Island. Doesn't Carl Miller own it? The guy who's behind Fortune Industries? I read an article about him in the newspaper the other day, something about him building a new factory somewhere overseas."

"Yes, he's the one."

"I thought so. By the way, were you at the house last night?"

Meg frowned. "Last night? No, I wasn't. Why?"

"I saw a light on the second floor. We didn't get our newspaper last night, and Stan thought the new delivery person might have left it at your house instead. I walked up your driveway, and, sure enough, spotted the paper. Then I saw the light."

A shiver rippled down Meg's spine. "I couldn't have been there; I was here on Gemini. I went to the house after Johnny and Alyssa's accident, but that was weeks ago. I was there during the day, and I didn't turn on any lights."

"I considered calling but decided the light had to be you, and if you wanted to talk, you'd call me. Now, I wish I had."

"I can't imagine how anyone would get in without setting off the alarm. This is worrisome." Meg's stomach tightened.

"I'll check later tonight and see if there's a light. If there is, I'll call you."

"Thanks, I'd appreciate your letting me know."

Meg and Davina said good-bye, promising to keep

in touch. After she hung up, Meg paced her living room, thinking about Davina's news. Last night, she suspected an intruder here in her cottage. Now, the house in Seattle may have been illegally entered as well.

Were the two incidents related? Did either or both have anything to do with the fatal accident? Whenever she thought of her daughter, her heart ached so badly she could hardly bear it. She wouldn't rest until she found out the truth.

If she sat here in her cottage, she'd never discover the answers to her questions. She must get out and look around, as she'd planned.

Now would be a good time to do some investigating. Carl was gone, and Eric and Lester were at the main house, deep in their discussion. She hated the idea of creeping around in the dark, but a glance out the window told her enough daylight lingered for at least half an hour's stroll.

She slipped into a light jacket and wound a printed silk scarf around her neck, to pull over her head in case the wind came up. Pocketing her keys to the cottage, she stepped outside and closed the door.

Instead of taking the path behind the cottage, she walked along the one in front. When she came to a fork in the path, she took the one to the left, which she hoped led to the beach. Overhead, the tops of the evergreen trees created a ragged silhouette against the gray sky. The thick woods could be either a protection or a menace. Tonight, they hemmed her in. She'd be glad when she reached the open spaces of the shore.

She soon discovered the path she'd chosen led to the docks. Uh oh, Burke and Jones were on one of the docks. Meg crept along, careful to not make noise that would attract their attention. Jones stood looking out to sea. Smoke from a cigarette stuck between his lips curled into the night air. Burke was hunkered down, checking the lines on a motorboat. His blond hair gleamed in the light cast from atop a post. The sound of their voices drifted along the airwaves, but she couldn't make out the words.

Meg slipped past them, looking over her shoulder to make sure they didn't turn and spot her. Then she headed toward Mt. Gemini. If she were careful—and lucky—Carl would never know she disobeyed his order to stay away from the far side of the island.

The low tide provided a generous beach. She hurried along, walking on the hard-packed sand near the shore, where she wouldn't leave footprints. Seagulls swooped overhead, landing to peck at tidbits the tide washed up. Their shrill caws echoed into the air. Bits of driftwood and kelp floated in and then back out again on the receding waves. In the distance, other islands appeared as silhouettes against the twilight sky.

A rustling sounded in the nearby bushes. Meg's breath fled her lungs. She peered ahead. Was someone there? Had Jones and Burke seen her after all and followed her?

Not Burke, but Eric. He burst from the bushes and jumped onto the sand. Dodging a pile of logs, he strode toward Meg, a big grin on his face. "We've got to stop meeting like this."

"Are you spying on me?" Meg propped her hands on her hips. Having him follow her was almost as bad as being discovered by Burke and Jones.

He drew back and raised his hands. "Of course

not."

"So what are you doing here?"

He shoved his hands in his jacket pockets. "I might ask you the same question. Seems to me you've ventured into off-limits territory."

She folded her arms. "Oh, really?"

"Yep. The mountain's up ahead, and it's my understanding we're not to go near it. You reminded me about Carl's warning earlier today."

Meg struggled to maintain her patience. "My understanding was he doesn't want us tramping through the woods where no developed paths run. He didn't say anything about not walking around the island by the beach."

His eyes flashed with admiration. "True, and a very good point. Mind if I come along, then?"

She tossed her head and resumed walking. "Suit yourself.

He fell into step beside her. "You left dinner early."

Was he checking up on her? "You and Lester were deep into your computer talk. I didn't think you'd miss me."

"Yeah, we were preoccupied. Sorry if you felt left out."

She waved a hand. "Never mind. What do you think of his big project for the Internet?"

"The program could work and make him a bundle. Or it could flop. I've seen projects like his go both ways. Even though the heyday of dot com millionaires is over, scoring big is still possible."

Meg stepped around a pile of seaweed. "Carl must believe in him, or he wouldn't back him."

"Carl seems to have a lot of money to spend on whatever."

"Like the museum."

"Yeah."

They rounded a corner and came up against a wall of boulders. Standing on tip-toes, Meg craned her neck but couldn't see over them. "Now what? I suppose you'll suggest we take to the water." She pointed to the water lapping against the outer edge of the wall.

He lifted a shoulder. "I'm game if you are. Don't you want to know what's on the other side?"

"Probably more of the same. The mountain's on the other side, though." She gazed at the purple cone rising above the pine trees. As she turned away, she saw something flash in the corner of her eye. She whirled and peered at the mountain again.

"What?" Eric studied her.

"I thought I saw a light just now. On top of the mountain." She focused on the dark pinnacle, and a few seconds later, a yellow light beamed into the night sky. The light lasted a few more seconds and then disappeared.

"There, did you see the light?" Meg looked at Eric.

He met her gaze and smiled. "I did. Good eye, Ms. Evans."

They waited, and, sure enough, the light beamed again. "What's going on?" Meg wondered aloud.

Eric stroked his chin and paced the sand. "Maybe the mountain functions as a lighthouse. Or is in the flight path to an airport.

"Maybe, but wouldn't Carl have mentioned it?"

Just then, the bushes rustled. Meg jumped and looked around. "Someone's coming!"

Eric ran to her. Grabbing the scarf around her neck, he pulled her close. "Put your arms around me."

Pulling back, she widened her eyes and stared. "What? Are you—?"

She meant to say "crazy," but his kiss silenced her. His lips were partly open, and he tasted of coffee and after-dinner liqueur. For one brief moment, she wanted to put her arms around him and lean into his body, as he had commanded.

Then she came to her senses. What was she thinking? Moreover, what was *he* thinking? She stiffened, raised both hands, and shoved against his chest. He held her like a vise.

"Hey!" someone called.

Looking over Eric's shoulder, Meg glimpsed a man running toward them. Moonlight glistened on spiky blond hair and caught the edge of a silver earring, outlined a snake tattoo on his thick, bare arm.

Burke. Meg tensed. She'd been so careful earlier to sneak by him and Jones at the docks, but here he was anyway.

He lurched to a stop. "Whaddya think yer doin'?"

Easing his arms from around Meg, Eric turned and faced the other man. "Yo, Burke. What're we doing? Should be obvious. Bad timing, man." He chuckled.

Burke planted his fists on his hips and leaned forward, his bulbous nose only inches from Eric's. "I ain't talkin' 'bout that. Didn't Carl tell ya this part of the island's off limits?"

"Oh? We thought the inland part was a no-no, but walking along the shore was okay. Right, Meg?" Eric slipped his arm around her waist and drew her close.

Meg rubbed her burning lips. "Um, right."

"Anything to do with the mountain is off-limits." Burke growled and pointed at the distant peak. "Even this part." He swung his arm around and stabbed his forefinger at the sand. "It's dangerous."

"How so?" Eric asked.

"High tide could cut you off your return trip. Ya might get hurt. He don't want the liability. So move along." His eyes glinted, and he jerked a thumb over his shoulder.

Meg took a step back the way they'd come, but Eric's arm around her waist held her fast. "Eric…"

"Just a sec." Eric kept his gaze on Burke.

The two men stared at each other.

Tension filled the air. Meg waited with bated breath. All she needed tonight, on top of everything else, was a showdown between two Alpha males.

Finally, Eric broke the silence. "You want us to leave, but you're in the way, pal."

He was right. The tide had turned, and if they walked around Burke on the waterside, they'd wade in water up to their ankles. If they left by the inland side, they'd need to forge through a thicket of salal and fern.

Burke's eyes narrowed to slits. He curled his hand into a fist, sending a ripple of muscle all the way up his arm. The snake tattoo undulated. His shoulders bunched, and he shuffled his feet.

Meg's heartbeat raced. *Please don't get into a fight!*

Seconds ticked by. Then, with a grumble, Burke stepped to one side, allowing them room to pass.

"Thanks, buddy." Eric drew Meg forward.

Meg blew out a relieved breath. She waited until she and Eric were several yards down the beach, and then she risked a glance over her shoulder.

Arms folded, leaning against the rock wall, Burke watched and waited.

She turned back to Eric. "What was *that* all about?"

"What?"

She pursed her lips. "You know what I'm talking about. The showdown back there."

Eric shrugged. "No showdown. We were having a friendly conversation."

"Uh huh. Then why did I get the feeling you two were about to tear each other apart?" Meg idly watched two seagulls land in a tide pool and dip their bills into the water. Out to sea, as twilight deepened, passing boats turned on their running lights. The air was cooler now, too, as the sun sank toward the horizon.

"I don't know. Must be your active imagination."

Meg huffed. "And by the way, I didn't appreciate being kissed."

He chuckled. "Really? I could have sworn you liked it."

"I did not. You had no right…"

He raised a hand. "Okay, okay. I thought kissing you was a smart move. Kept him from thinking we were out snooping around."

"We weren't snooping. At least I wasn't. I was out for…for an evening walk."

"Whatever." A shoulder shrugged. "I still wanted to distract him. But, I apologize. Feel better now?"

She let a couple seconds elapse while she matched his steps around a pile of driftwood. The gulls from the tide pool swept by overhead, in search of more lucrative hunting. "Okay…apology accepted. Do you think

Burke was following us, or was he just making his rounds? I saw him and Jones at the docks earlier, but I'm sure they didn't see me."

"Hard to say. But I wouldn't worry about it, if I were you."

She drew herself up and lifted her chin. "Well, you're not me, are you?"

"Hey, don't get mad." He raised both hands." I don't know Burke's agenda. He probably patrols here every night."

Meg hopped to one side to avoid a ring of kelp and seaweed. "Do you really think Carl doesn't want anyone on this part of the island because of liability?"

"Do you?" Eric countered.

The man infuriated her. "Oh, never mind!"

They lapsed into silence.

When they reached their cottages, Eric placed a hand on her arm. "How about a drink at my place? You look like you could use one, and I know I sure could. I found a nice bottle of Scotch in my kitchen cupboard..."

Meg bit her lower lip. A drink might be just what she needed after the unnerving encounter with Burke. Then Eric's kiss on the beach flashed through her mind. Feeling his warm lips on hers, and how she'd wanted to melt into him and kiss him back. The man was trouble. Big trouble.

She swallowed hard and pulled away. "Thanks, but I think I'll call it a night."

A shadow flitted across his face, but then he smiled and shrugged. "Okay, see you tomorrow."

****

Inside her cottage, Meg climbed the stairs to the

loft. In the bathroom, she washed her face and while patting her skin dry, gazed in the mirror. She focused on her lips, unable to get Eric's kiss out of her mind.

What was it about the man that kept the tension humming through her veins when she was with him? And kept him in her thoughts even when they were apart? She had no interest in a new romantic relationship. Not because she still had feelings for Johnny—her love for him died long ago. She wasn't ready to trust another man, or to love again.

Even if she were, she would not choose Eric Richards. They had nothing in common and had been thrown together only temporarily. No matter how this island sojourn turned out, they would end up going their separate ways.

Meg brushed her teeth and went into the bedroom. Before climbing into bed, she crossed to the window and gazed out. She studied the mountain peak for several minutes, but no light appeared. If the light she and Eric saw earlier were a mariner's warning beacon, as he suggested, wouldn't the light flash throughout the night?

Her gaze dropped to Eric's cottage. Bands of light seeped through a first floor window's shuttered blinds. He was probably having his drink. She pictured him relaxing on his sofa, feet propped up, and glass in hand.

Regret filled her. They both were alone. If she had accepted his offer, they could have been company for each other, for a little while, at least.

No, better to be alone than to court danger by keeping company with Eric Richards.

****

Eric finished his Scotch-on-the-rocks and set the

glass in the sink. The taste of the alcohol lingered pleasantly on his tongue. He switched off the light and climbed the stairs to his loft. So much for investigating the island this evening. After dinner, thinking Meg safely tucked away in her cottage, he'd headed for the mountain. When he spotted Meg, he decided to join her, rather than risk running into her later, when he might have come across something important.

Then Burke appeared, and Eric did the first thing he thought of to throw the other man off. He pretended he and Meg were making out.

Now, though, he wondered if his action wasn't an excuse to kiss her, an urge he'd had since they'd met. Okay, had he satisfied his curiosity? Her lips were warm and soft, her body tight against his. She could deny it until hell froze, but he knew without a doubt she *had* kissed him back.

Guilt nagged him. He already had a girlfriend. Sort of. Sally Marshall was a programmer for a tech company he did business with. Engrossed with her career, she had no desire to be saddled with a relationship, much less marriage and children.

He and Sally got together once or twice a month. Either he would call her or she him. If the one being called was not available, neither had hurt feelings. When they did get together, the purpose was strictly to have a good time. They understood each other, and the arrangement was perfect for them both.

He had a feeling Meg was a different kind of woman. Yep, he'd better watch himself, or he'd be in deep trouble where Meg Evans was concerned.

Chapter Seven

Meg sat by the pool watching Laureen and two women helpers imported from Orcas Island set up a buffet lunch on a long table. Today was Friday and, as Carl had promised, his weekend guests were arriving. They checked into their respective cottages and now Burke and Jones were bringing them back to the main house.

So far, none of the guests appeared familiar, but as Meg scanned the man alighting from Burke's cart, she recognized Kent Gheller.

He turned to offer his hand to a blonde woman who looked to be in her twenties. White shorts showed off her shapely tan legs, and a low-cut blue blouse revealed a hint of cleavage. Was she his wife? If so, she was a trophy wife. Kent Gheller was at least fifty.

Meg stood and waved to Gheller.

He caught her eye and nodded. Whispering to his companion, he grasped her elbow and guided her to Meg.

She stepped forward to meet them halfway. "Nice to see you again, Mr. Gheller."

"Hello, Meg. Why don't you call me Kent?"

"All right."

Kent's clipped beard defined his pointed chin. His eyes and his mouth drooped at the corners, giving him a sad look. He'd appeared unhappy during her interview, but she thought something temporary had upset him. Now, she suspected sadness might be his usual demeanor.

"This is Helen Wilson." Kent gestured to his companion. "She does all Carl's PR."

Helen Wilson held out her hand. "So you're Meg Evans."

Helen's tone indicated she'd heard about Meg. "Do I know you?" As she shook Helen's hand, Meg studied her. The woman didn't look at all familiar. However, Helen was older than she'd at first thought, probably somewhere in her thirties.

Helen stepped aside to allow a couple to pass by and then turned back to Meg. "Ah, no, we don't know each other. Kent mentioned your name on the way here. Didn't you, Kent?

"I probably did." He shrugged his narrow shoulders. "How's the job going, Meg?"

"Good. I like working with the artifacts."

Kent frowned. "I understand you have someone working with you. I wasn't aware Carl was hiring anyone else."

"Yes, his name is Eric Richards."

"Is he here?" Kent pulled his gaze away from Meg to scan the area.

"He's the one over there talking to Carl." She pointed to the other end of the pool, where the two men were deep in conversation.

"I'd like to meet him."

Just then, Carl moved off to greet more new arrivals, and Eric looked around. His gaze lighted on Meg. She waved him over, and when he joined them, she introduced Helen first.

Helen held out her hand and beamed a wide smile. "Nice to meet you."

"Same here."

Eric clasped Helen's hand, and the two gazed at each other.

Meg felt her stomach tighten. "This is Kent Gheller," she said in a rush. "The man who interviewed and hired me."

Eric finally dropped Helen's hand and turned to Kent. "Nice to meet you, Kent."

The two men began talking but their words didn't penetrate Meg's mind. She was busy analyzing her reaction to Eric and Helen.

You're jealous.

Ridiculous. She had no interest in Eric. None whatsoever. And she certainly had no claim on him, not even after kissing him. Wait, she hadn't kissed him. *He'd* kissed *her—*

"Meg?"

Helen's voice broke into Meg's thoughts. "Sorry, what?"

"I asked if you'd been in the pool yet." She nodded toward the swimming pool where several guests were already testing the water.

"Ah, no. I've been looking forward to it, though."

"Me, too. Think I'll go change and take a dip now. Why don't you join me? Or us, if I can convince these two to stop talking business and relax." She laid a hand on Kent's arm. "Come on, guys. Let's do something fun."

****

When Meg arrived back at the pool, she saw Helen poised to enter the water by the concrete stairs at the shallow end. Of course, she looked great in her blue, one-piece suit with the sides cut up to her waist.

The men were already in the water. Kent lounged against the side of the pool, bony elbows resting on the tiles, water dripping from his beard. Sunglasses hid his sad eyes.

Eric waded to the steps and reached up to assist Helen.

Helen grasped Eric's hand, stepped daintily down the steps, and into the water.

When Meg came along, Eric again reached out.

Ignoring his gesture, she gripped the railing. "No, thanks. I'll manage." She stepped down onto the first step, slipped, lost her grip on the rail, and plunged into the pool. She sank below the surface and came up sputtering water.

Eric tossed back his head and laughed, but then he sobered and swam toward her. "Are you okay?"

"Of course, I'm okay." Turning her back, she swam away.

Eric and Helen joined several other guests in tossing a large red ball. Kent stayed where he was, watching rather than participating.

Meg chose not to join in, either, but instead swam languidly around in small circles at the free end of the pool. The cool water refreshed her. Finally, she climbed from the pool, grabbed a towel, and headed for a pink-cushioned chaise lounge. She lay back, closed her eyes, and let the warm sun soak into her skin. The sounds of laughter and the clink of ice in glasses as the guests enjoyed their cocktails swirled around her.

"Mind if I join you?"

Meg opened her eyes to see Helen, a towel

wrapped around her slender waist, water dripping from the ends of her shoulder-length hair. "Not at all. Have a seat." Meg waved at the empty chaise lounge next to hers.

Helen settled onto the chaise, leaning back and stretching out her long legs. Beads of water glistened on her tanned skin. "Whew, that was a workout."

"I know. I swam for a while but got tired and had to quit."

Laureen approached, the sun reflecting brightly off her white slacks and tunic top, and asked if they wanted anything from the portable bar, where Burke, as usual, mixed the drinks.

"I'll have a glass of white wine," Meg said.

Helen waved a hand. "Burke knows what I like. Just tell him who it's for."

Laureen went off to place their orders, and Meg turned to Helen. "So, you've been here often."

"Because Burke knows what I drink?" Helen leaned back against the cushions. "Yes, I have. Carl is famous for his parties. He loves to entertain."

"Is he married?" Meg had wondered, but she hadn't been brave enough to ask him. Her gaze caught their host now, moving from guest to guest like a politician working the room at a political rally. Hand outstretched, big smile, lots of backslapping.

Helen picked up her towel and dried the ends of her hair. "No, he never was. And no, he's not gay. He says he's not cut out for marriage. He has a special woman friend, Darla Costas. She's an actress. Maybe you've heard of her."

Meg nodded. "She starred in a play I saw at The Rep."

"Uh huh. I expect she'll be here, eventually. But what about you? Are you married?"

"Divorced. You?"

"I'm still looking for Mr. Right." Her gaze strayed to the pool.

Helen's laugh sounded forced. Meg checked to see what held her attention. The pool was empty now, except for Eric, lazily swimming laps. He stopped and swiped the water from his eyes. He looked their way, grinned, and gave a salute.

"Eric seems nice." Helen cast Meg a sideways look. "Are you and he…?"

Meg flicked her hand as though brushing away a troublesome fly. "Heavens, no. We only work together. We met a few days ago when Jones picked us up on Orcas. But what about Kent?"

"He has a wife."

"Did she come to the party?"

Helen grabbed a cushion from a nearby chair and stuck it behind her head. "No. She's not much for parties. She's from Sukarla. The Middle Eastern country where a war is going on?"

Meg nodded. The war in Sukarla, in which the United States was involved, had dominated the news for the past few months.

Helen sat up and leaned toward Meg. Her hair, almost dry now, swung forward like a curtain. "Kent told me all her family over there were killed," she said in subdued tones. "She would have been killed, too, because she was visiting, but she got out just before the war started."

"That was lucky."

"Wasn't it? Kent adores her. You should see them

together."

"Really?" Meg swung her glance toward Kent. "He doesn't seem the overly demonstrative type."

Helen leaned back again and adjusted the cushion behind her head. "He is where she's concerned."

"Kent seems very intense about his job."

"Oh, yes. He works hard for Carl. We all do."

Laureen arrived with their drinks, and Helen turned away to pluck hers from the tray.

****

Ready for dinner, Meg stepped off the path and onto the patio at the main house. After the sumptuous brunch, she thought she'd never be hungry again, but the hours she'd put in at the museum this afternoon had whetted her appetite.

Most of the guests were already seated at the round tables, and Eric and Helen sat together. Wearing a strapless yellow dress, Helen sipped a drink in a tall glass with a tiny paper umbrella. Eric, in jeans and a short-sleeved brown shirt, drank his beer from the bottle.

The remaining places at their table were empty, but Meg turned in the opposite direction. No way would she join them. Let them spend the entire evening together. Who cared? She had no claim on Eric. Didn't want to have. So what if he paid attention to Helen?

She joined the line at the buffet table. The array of food looked and smelled wonderful, and she filled her plate with roasted chicken, couscous, tossed salad, and fresh fruit. Spying Carl's computer expert, she sat with Lester. Also at his table was a middle-aged couple, Addie and Norm Bolton. In matching Hawaiian print shirts and khaki slacks, they might have been twins, but for their difference in size. While Addie was petite and thin, Norm was burly with a stomach the size of a beach ball.

"So what do you two do for Fortune Industries?" Meg asked as she lifted her fork.

"Norm is Carl's Director of Overseas Operations," Addie announced, her eyes gleaming with pride. She smoothed her dyed red hair, jingling her charm bracelet.

"Is that right?" Interested in learning more, Meg turned to Norm.

His mouth stuffed with food, Norm nodded.

"Norm's gone a lot." Addie cut into her chicken drumstick. "But I'm glad he was here for Carl's party. I love Carl's parties, and I hate to attend alone." She leaned toward Meg. "Are you here alone, dear?"

Meg finished a bite of salad, savoring the tangy dressing. "Yes. I'm here for a few weeks cataloging Carl's artifacts."

Addie wrinkled her nose. "Working in Carl's stuffy old museum."

"The work is interesting.

"If you like that sort of thing." Addie grinned. "I'm more a people person."

Lester waved his knife. "Watch out for her, Meg. She'll have you matched up with someone before you know it."

Lester was dressed in denim, as usual, with his black-framed eyeglasses perched precariously on his thin nose. His hair still resembled a bird's nest, but Meg had decided the look was intentional, rather than accidental.

Addie frowned at Lester. "All except you."

Lester put his knife to work layering butter on a

piece of sourdough bread. "I already have a girlfriend."

"So you say." Addie sniffed. "I've never seen her."

"Doesn't mean she doesn't exist. She lives in Canada."

"That's not far away from here. You should've invited her to the party. Carl wouldn't mind."

"She's busy this weekend." Lester took a generous bite of the bread.

"I like to see people happy, like I am." Addie favored Norm with an affectionate look.

"Addie means well," Norm said before shoveling in a forkful of potato salad.

"I do." His wife nodded. "You're gone so much, and with the kids grown and living away, I need something to keep me occupied."

Meg made a dismissive wave. "Don't waste your time on me. I'm not looking for anyone."

Sipping from her glass, Addie raised her eyebrows. "Bad marriage?"

Meg looked down at her plate. "Yes, as it turned out."

"Now, Addie, don't pry," Norm cautioned with a narrowed gaze.

"I'm not." Addie pushed out her lower lip. "I'm just making conversation. Besides, I have others I'm working for."

"Working on, you mean," Lester said. "Like Helen Wilson."

Addie shook her head. "Poor Helen. She recently lost her love. He passed away. I don't even know who he was or what he died from."

"Oh?" Addie's revelation piqued Meg's curiosity, and she glanced to where the woman sat.

"He died while we were on our trip to Saudi." Addie touched her napkin to her lips. "When the weather got unbearable, I came home to find Helen in mourning. When I attempted to comfort her, she said she didn't want to talk about it."

"She looks like she's recovering pretty good now." Lester nodded to the table where Helen and Eric sat, their heads together and laughing like old friends.

Addie smacked her lips. "My, my, who *is* the delicious-looking man with Helen?"

"An expert Carl imported to help with his precious artifacts," Lester said.

"His name is Eric Richards," Meg supplied. "He's also a computer software consultant, or something like that." She wasn't exactly certain about Eric's profession.

"He is definitely too handsome to be shut up in a musty old museum." Addie chuckled.

"Hey, Addie," Norm said. "Give it a rest, huh?"

She smiled and patted his arm. "Norm, you just never mind. This promises to be a very interesting party."

****

Later that night, Meg finished brushing her hair and then stepped from the bathroom into her loft bedroom. Before climbing into bed, she gave in to her curiosity and glanced out the window toward Eric's cottage. Except for the light on the porch, the place was dark.

After dinner, the partying at Carl's had continued, with guests gathering around the pool for after-dinner drinks and conversation. Meg stayed for a while, but having no one in particular to chat with, she soon took her leave. Judging by his dark cottage, Eric chose to stay. Keeping Helen company, no doubt.

Meg finally settled in bed, read for a while, dozed off, and then woke up. She went into the bathroom for a drink of water. *I will not look out to see if Eric is home yet.* Still, on the way back from the bathroom, she detoured to the window. His cottage lay in darkness. Well, he and Helen must be having a really good time. Not that she cared.

****

Eric stood in the shadows outside his cottage. The hour was late, but he would phone Nick anyway. The sooner his friend hunted up the information he wanted, the better. He switched on his cell phone and punched the illuminated keys.

"Hey, man," said a sleepy-sounding Nick.

Eric winced. "Sorry to call so late, but I have a few more people for you to check out."

"Sure, sure."

"Got paper and pencil?"

A few minutes later, after inquiring about Nick's wife and hearing she was okay, Eric rang off.

As he clipped his phone to his belt, he glanced at Meg's cottage. All was dark. He'd seen her leave the party and wanted to accompany her home but hadn't been able to get away from Helen Wilson. The woman had a very persistent come-on. He wasn't interested, but she might know something that would aid his investigation. Even though he'd been on Gemini only a few days, he needed to make progress before time ran out.

Chapter Eight

The following morning, Carl's actress friend, Darla Costas, arrived. Dressed in a white blouse, an ankle-length, blue skirt, and with a circlet of daisies atop her dark, waist-length hair, she might have come directly from the stage.

Carl introduced her to everyone at lunch.

"I've seen you in plays at The Rep," Meg said, when her turn came.

Darla's wide smile showed even, white teeth. "Yes, I've been with the company for several years. Right now, I'm playing Kate in *The Taming of the Shrew.*"

Carl put his arm around Darla's waist and gave her a hug. "I'm trying to talk her into giving us a sample sometime this weekend."

Darla laughed. "He always wants me to perform. But of course. I will."

"I look forward to that." Meg clasped her hands in anticipation.

They chatted for a couple more minutes, and then Carl said, "Oh, by the way, Meg, I want you and Eric to take a break this afternoon while I give everyone a tour of the museum. Go for a swim or just relax. We'll all join you later."

Meg warmed to his suggestion. "Why, thanks, Carl. Some free time would be a treat."

"How about it?" Eric asked Meg a few minutes

later. "Are you up for a swim?"

Meg shook her head. "I plan to rest in my cottage. I'm not used to all this partying."

"Okay, I've got phone calls to make. See you later."

Was it her imagination, or had he look relieved?

At Wolf House, Meg busied herself with housekeeping chores for half an hour, which she figured would be time enough for the museum tour to be underway, and then she left, taking the path back to the main house. With everyone at the museum, now would be a good time to look around Carl's office. Time on the island was passing, and, so far, she hadn't found out anything about Johnny and why someone may have purposely caused his and Aly's accident.

With Laureen still in the house, and Burke and Jones lurking who knew where, investigating would be risky. But, as the saying went, nothing ventured, nothing gained. If she met with questions, she'd say she was looking for a sweater she mislaid at lunch.

As she neared the house, Meg spotted Laureen on the patio, cleaning up from lunch. Waiting until the woman's back was turned, Meg slipped by and hurried to the back door of the house. She went inside and, keeping her back straight and her head high, strode down the hallway.

The door to Carl's office stood ajar. Her heartbeat quickened. She hesitated, her courage seeping away like a tire with a leak. Was she crazy? What if she got caught?

Then she thought of Aly and the horrible accident that took her young life. A lump formed in her throat. "I'm doing this for you, Aly," she whispered. She straightened her shoulders and slipped inside the room.

Stopping inside the door, she looked around to get her bearings. The drawn blinds gave everything a brownish cast. The spacious office had the usual desk, computer, printer, filing cabinets and bookshelves. A sofa, overstuffed chairs, and a coffee table added homey touches.

The desk would be a good place to begin. She crept toward it and then stopped short. Someone sat in Carl's leather swivel chair, working on the computer. The person must be Lester. She couldn't think of anyone else who might freely use Carl's machine. Darn, she'd forgotten about him.

Reason told her to turn around and quietly leave. But she was curious to know for certain the person's identity. She inched closer, leaning sideways to see a profile and thus identify him. Or her.

Thick brown hair, high forehead, strong, straight nose, firm chin.

Eric.

Meg gasped. Then, without thinking through the consequences, she blurted, "What are you doing here?"

He twisted his head in her direction and dropped his jaw. Then he leaned back in the swivel chair and drawled, "I might ask you the same thing."

His tone was as cool as the air flowing from the room's air conditioner. She lifted her chin. "I'm looking for my sweater. I left it here at lunchtime."

He raised one eyebrow. "In Carl's office? I doubt that."

"But you're into his computer. What are you looking for?" She marched forward and peered at the screen where a chart was displayed.

Eric stabbed a key and the chart disappeared, replaced by a screen saver montage of totem poles. "I wanted to check out something on the Internet."

Meg's instincts told her he was lying. She'd been suspicious of him from the beginning. First had been the longboat that he, the so-called expert, had fumbled to identify. Then the Tlingit face mask. Then she'd run into him roaming the island and suspected he was armed. Innocently exploring his new home? Or on some other mission? "I think you're lying," she said with a boldness that amazed her. "Unless you tell me what you're really doing, I'll tell Carl you were here."

Eric folded his arms. "Don't we sound high and mighty."

"Who are you? I don't think you're the expert you pretend to be."

"And what do you think Carl would say if he knew who *you* are? And that you're here to spy on him."

Meg pressed a hand to her chest and stepped back. She hadn't expected him to return her challenge with one of his own. "W-what are you talking about? I'm not spying!"

He leaped from the chair, sending it spinning, and strode to her. The air between them crackled. "Then why are you here, Mrs. Johnny Stanton? Okay, ex-Mrs. Stanton."

Pulse racing, Meg stared. "You know about Johnny and me?"

"If you thought you could hide behind your maiden name, you were wrong." He stuck his hands on his hips. "Now, want to tell me about it?"

Okay, so he knew her true identity. She wasn't about to cave in. Standing tall, she lifted her chin. "Not unless you tell me what you're doing and why you're on the island."

Eric scowled. He paced to the window and stood with feet planted apart and his back to her. The tension radiating from him was palpable.

Meg chewed her lower lip. Had she made a grave mistake by calling his bluff?

Finally, he wheeled around. "You win," he growled. "We'll talk. But not here."

"Then where?"

"Somewhere off the island." He stroked his chin. "We'll wait until the party breaks up tomorrow and everyone's leaving. We'll say we want to go shopping...on Orcas Island."

Knowing he too had secrets to keep from Carl gave Meg new courage. "I don't want to go shopping. I don't want to go anywhere with you."

He made a fist and pounded his palm. "Too bad. We're stuck with each other now."

"Stuck? What do you mean?"

Down the hall, a door slammed.

"We need to get out of here. Now." Eric grabbed her arm and dragged her toward the office door.

Meg trotted along beside Eric down the hallway toward the back door. Fortunately, they encountered no one. Still, he didn't release her arm until they were outside and on one of the paths leading away from the house.

"Here's the plan," he said, his tone stern. "We're going back to our cottages, put on our swimsuits, and be waiting by the pool when Carl and the others return from the museum. Got it?"

She shook her head. "No. I told him I planned to

read, not swim."

"Doesn't matter. We want him to think we were keeping each other company."

Meg opened her mouth to reply, but just then, only yards away, Jones stepped from the bushes and onto the path. She clamped her jaw shut.

"Hey, you two!" Ponytail swaying, Jones strode toward them.

Eric's lips grazed Meg's ear. "I'll do the talking."

The memory of encountering Burke on the beach flashed before her eyes. "Don't you dare kiss me this time," she whispered back.

"I'll play it as I see it." He grinned and slung his arm around her shoulder. "Yo, Jones."

"Everyone's supposed to be at the museum." Jones narrowed his eyes.

"Not us. Carl told us to chill a while." Eric smirked.

Jones stuck out his chin and planted his hands on his hips. "I don't think so."

Eric shrugged. "Ask him."

Jones focused his black-eyed gaze on Meg.

Now is your chance. Tell him what Eric was doing in Carl's office.

"Isn't that what Carl said, Meg?" Eric dug his fingers into her shoulder.

Meg sucked in her breath. Indecision hung over her like a guillotine waiting to fall. Damned if she did, damned if she didn't.

"Meg?" Eric prompted.

Jones' black-eyed gaze bored into her.

What to do, what to do? "Um…right." She pasted on a smile.

"Carl don't like it when people don't do what he says," Jones said. "This is twice now."

"Twice?" Eric raised his eyebrows.

"Burke says the other night you was walkin' where you wasn't supposed to be."

"We didn't know Carl meant to keep off that part of the beach," Eric said. "I thought Burke understood."

"Don't matter. You was still where you weren't supposed to be."

"So what? Three strikes, and we're out?" Eric laughed.

Jones set his jaw. A tense silence hung in the air.

Was this another male standoff? Meg gritted her teeth.

Finally, Jones heaved a breath. "Don't say I didn't warn you." He turned and stomped off toward the main house.

Meg expected Eric to call out a last word. Thankfully, he clamped his jaw shut instead. Keeping his arm around her, he drew them along the path.

Meg followed but glanced over her shoulder at Jones. As soon as he disappeared around a bend, she jerked away from Eric. "Do you think he believed what you told him about us getting sidetracked?"

"Why wouldn't he?"

"Because…because you spent all last evening with Helen Wilson."

His eyes glinted. "You noticed."

"In passing."

"Do I detect a note of jealousy?"

Meg stuck her nose in the air. "Absolutely not. I was merely poking holes in your attempt to fool Jones about our supposed interest in each other. I don't think your plan worked."

"Don't worry. I don't underestimate him." He leaned forward. "And I had a reason for spending time with Helen."

"Which is?" She clapped a hand over her mouth. "None of my business."

"Maybe, maybe not. But you'll have to wait until tomorrow to find out."

****

The following day dragged. All Meg could think about was the talk she and Eric were to have. She hoped she hadn't made a mistake by agreeing to leave the island with him.

As a party finale, Darla, aided by a male guest, gave a rousing performance from *The Taming of the Shrew*. Her Kate was superb, everyone agreed, and they gave the two performers a hearty round of applause.

The group broke up, and Eric appeared at Meg's side. "We're all set to go to Orcas. I told Carl we needed some personal things we forgot to bring along."

"I'm surprised he agreed. He's fussy about everyone staying together."

"I have the key to *Wave Catcher* to prove it." He held up a metal ring dangling a key. "Come on. We'll get a head start before the others leave."

At the docks, they found *Wave Catcher,* a motorboat with a fiberglass top, painted white with yellow trim, and large enough to have a cabin complete with galley and bunks.

Eric climbed aboard and reached out to help Meg.

She looked at his outstretched hand and hesitated, her stomach tensing. Did she really want to go with him? When she stepped into the boat, she would be putting her life in his hands.

"Hurry up," Eric urged. "Here comes Burke. No, don't look around. Act natural. Come on. Now."

Meg took a deep breath, put her hand in his, and leaped aboard. Once her feet were planted on the deck, she freed herself from his grasp and turned toward shore. Sure enough, Burke lumbered along the dock toward them. He wore his usual uniform of sleeveless T-shirt and ragged-hemmed jeans. His square-jawed face reflected a combination of curiosity and wariness.

"Where ya goin'?" he called.

"Orcas," Eric replied. "Do a little shopping."

Burke stopped and glared. "Who said ya could?"

"Got the key from Carl himself." Eric dangled the key from thumb and forefinger.

"You know how to operate the boat?"

"Sure do. Grew up around boats. How 'bout giving us a hand?" Eric pointed to one of the ropes tied around a dock cleat.

Burke scowled and kept his feet firmly planted.

Eric lifted his chin and squared his shoulders.

Tension thickened the air. Meg inwardly rolled her eyes.

Finally, Burke squatted in front of the cleat and untied the rope. He tossed the rope to Eric and then freed the remaining rope as well.

Soon the motor hummed and Eric steered the boat away from the dock. "See ya!" he yelled to Burke.

Meg forced a smile and waved.

Hands on his hips, Burke gave a curt nod.

"Geesh, he's a pain," Eric said when they were well out of the man's earshot.

"He's just doing his job."

"Okay, but does he have to be so obnoxious and arrogant about it?"

Meg could have told him Burke wasn't the only one being obnoxious and arrogant, but she kept her mouth shut.

Eric twisted the wheel to avoid a drifting log. "Soon as we get to Orcas, we'll talk. For now, sit and relax." He nodded to the seat opposite his.

She hopped onto the high perch where she could see through the windshield. The surrounding islands as well as several passing sailboats were outlined against a clear blue sky, and the water was calm. But relax? Hardly. Her nerves were strung as tight as steel wire. So many questions needed answers, and she still had misgivings about throwing in her lot with Eric.

She shifted her gaze to him. Rather than occupy the captain's seat, he stood at the helm. With his broad shoulders and strong arms, and long legs planted firmly on the deck, he made a striking figure. Under wind-tossed hair, his profile, with high forehead, straight nose, and well-defined chin, suggested strength and determination.

Focusing on his mouth, she recalled the crush of his lips against hers, and a sudden, searing heat filled her. Not wanting to be attracted to this man she didn't fully trust, she shook off the disturbing feeling. "Which part of the island are we going to?"

Eric kept his gaze on the water. "Eastsound."

"Not where the ferry dock is?"

"No, and not because I'm afraid you'd try to hop aboard one and escape."

"What makes you so sure I wouldn't?"

"Because you're curious to know what I have to

say." He cast her a sly glance. "And, you like me."

She dropped her jaw. "In your dreams!"

Eric burst into laughter. "I knew that would get a rise out of you."

Meg turned away and looked out the windshield again, determined not to say another word until they reached their destination.

Chapter Nine

Twenty minutes later, they cruised into East Sound, the long neck of water that nearly divided Orcas Island into two separate pieces of land. Eric slowed the engine, and the boat's nose lowered to the water.

Meg gazed at the elaborate homes hidden among the trees, hideaways for the rich and, in some cases, the famous as well.

They reached the public dock at the village of Eastsound and tied the boat fast. Climbing the staircase to the shore brought a flood of memories. Years ago, she and Johnny and Alyssa, then a toddler, had vacationed on Orcas, staying at the famous Rosario Resort. Tears welled behind her eyes. She and Johnny had been so happy, so in love. And they'd had their wonderful child.

Now all she had were loneliness and an aching heart. Would she ever recover from her loss? Would she ever find out the truth about what had happened to Johnny and Alyssa? Or was this interlude on Gemini a wild goose chase?

Putting aside her worries, she focused on the present. Now the height of the tourist season, Eastsound burgeoned with visitors. People were everywhere, taking pictures, sampling the cuisine of the various restaurants, and visiting the shops.

Eric knew his way around and without discussion

led them to a corner restaurant with an outdoor eating area. They sat at an umbrella-shaded, wrought iron table surrounded by wooden barrels of begonias, pansies, and geraniums.

A waiter appeared with glasses of ice water and took their order. Meg requested a cup of mint tea and a cranberry muffin, and Eric a beer.

"Nice place, isn't it?" Eric said. "Reminds me of a restaurant I once ate at in London. Ever been there?"

She pursed her lips. "No, I haven't. But let's get down to business, shall we? This isn't exactly a...social occasion." She'd almost said "date" but stopped herself in time.

"All right, business it is. What do you want to know?"

"Start with what you know about me."

He sipped his water and then leaned back in his chair. "Okay, I know your ex-husband was a man named Johnny Stanton. He was an accountant for a company contracted by Fortune Industries. He was an alcoholic. You split up. He went to rehab. He died in a car accident while under the influence."

He rattled off the facts as though he were reading a newspaper. Meg gasped and pressed a hand to her chest. "You found out a lot about me, didn't you?"

"I have good sources."

"So what if all you say is true?"

"Not *if*. It is true." He narrowed his eyes. "And I find it a little too coincidental you just happen to be working for Carl now."

Meg tapped her fingers on the tabletop. "Wait a minute. I was the one who found you in Carl's office. You're the one who owes *me* an explanation.

He dismissed her challenge with a wave of his hand. "No, if I owe anyone, the person would be Carl. But he doesn't know I was there. Besides, his office was your destination, too." He leaned forward and pinned her with a stern look. "Wasn't it?"

He'd hit a sore spot. She bit her lip and looked away. Then she took a deep breath. "You know all about me, and I know nothing about you. It's only fair you tell me something before I reveal any more."

He took a sip of water, steadily eyeing her, and then set the glass on the paper coaster. "You've got a point. But what I'm about to say goes no farther than right here. Understood?"

She spread her hands. "How can I make such a promise? What if you share something I need to tell Carl?"

"You either give me your word, or it's no go."

Meg heaved a disgusted sigh. "All right."

The waiter arrived with their orders.

Meg dipped the tea bag into her cup of hot water then sliced off a portion of her muffin and spread it with butter.

Ignoring the glass that came with his beer, Eric took a long swig from the bottle. He leaned forward again and lowered his voice. "I'm here because I think something illegal is going on at Gemini. I want to find out what it is."

"Illegal?" She widened her eyes. "Like what?"

"That's what I'm here to find out."

"Don't you have any clues? Does it have to do with Carl's collection? With his museum?"

He shrugged. "Maybe. I don't know."

Meg ate a bite of muffin. Still warm from the oven

and tangy with cranberries, the bread melted in her mouth. "Maybe he's selling fake Indian artifacts. But why? He seems wealthy enough."

Eric frowned. "Whatever's happening may not be Carl's doing, although I don't see how something could go on without his knowledge. Gemini is his island, after all."

Two pigeons hopped along the sidewalk. Meg broke off a bit of her muffin and tossed it to them. "Maybe it has to do with the mountain and the off-limits part of the island."

"Very possibly."

They both fell silent. The pigeons strutted, cocking their heads, looking hopeful.

Meg tossed them a few more crumbs. Finally, she looked up. "That's all you're sharing?"

He nodded. "Your turn."

"Really? Already?"

"Hey, this was your idea."

"All right." Meg took a sip of tea. "I don't believe Johnny's death was an accident. Yes, he was an alcoholic, but he'd been in rehab and was serious about recovering. He wouldn't have mixed a codeine cold medicine with the drug he took for his alcoholism. I believe someone drugged him. Someone who wanted him to have an accident that would kill him."

"So, what exactly brought you to Gemini Island?"

Meg's throat tightened. "Right before the, ah, the accident, he phoned. I wasn't home, and he left a message on my answering machine. All he said was, 'It's under Gemini, Meg. Remember that. Under Gemini.' When I found out Carl Miller owns Gemini Island, and knowing Johnny worked for him, I thought

Carl's island might be the Gemini Johnny was talking about. Taking the job and coming here was a long shot, but I had no other leads. I felt so helpless and frustrated." She threw up her hands.

Eric's eyes lighted. "This is really interesting. What led you here is similar to why I came." He took a swig of beer and set down the bottle. "A friend of mine, a young Nootlinga woman named Norrie, called me one night and said she wanted to tell me something. Could I come to her house on the res? When I got there, I found her unconscious. Drug paraphernalia all over the place. While we waited for the ambulance, she opened her eyes and spoke." He stopped and ran a hand through his hair.

Meg leaned forward. "What did she say?"

"She said, 'Gemini Island. It's under Gemini.'"

Meg gasped. "Similar to what Johnny said. Only he didn't add the 'island.' If he had, he would've saved me some research."

"But they both said, 'It's under Gemini.'"

"Yes. But what happened to your friend? Did she recover?"

He looked away and ran a hand over his face. "She died. The coroner said from a drug overdose."

"Oh, I'm...I'm so sorry." Meg pressed her fingers to her lips.

He acknowledged her sentiment with a brief nod. "The thing is, she'd been to rehab and had promised to keep clean."

"Again, just like Johnny." A chill spread over Meg, and she hugged her arms.

"I think Norrie knew something somebody didn't want her to know—or to tell. They killed her by faking a drug overdose. The same could be true of Johnny."

Ah, they'd both come to the same conclusion. "What about your friend's relatives? What do they think?"

"Both her parents are dead. There are other relatives, but they're scattered around. No one has any particular interest in her. Her dad was a good buddy of mine. I promised him I'd look out for her. I let him down."

Meg reached out. "You can't blame yourself."

He clenched his hands into fists. "But I do blame myself. That's why I must find out the truth. I owe it to her, and to her parents."

"That's the way I feel, too." Tears welled, and before she could blink them back, they trickled down her cheeks. She turned away her face.

"You still love him."

She shook her head. "No."

"Then what? There's something else." Reaching into his back jeans' pocket, he pulled out a handkerchief and held it toward her.

"Thanks." Her fingers brushed his as she took the cloth. She dabbed at her cheeks, conscious of the faint smell of aftershave. "Our daughter, Alyssa, was in the back seat of the car. He picked her up from the hospital after she broke her leg roller-skating. She died in the accident, too." Meg's chest tightened. "That's another reason I think someone drugged Johnny. He never would have risked Aly's life by knowingly mixing drugs."

Eric's mouth fell open. "Oh, man, I didn't know about your daughter. I'm so sorry." He reached across the table and grasped her hand.

She leaned toward him, aching to be in his arms, to be comforted and soothed. "Thank you," she whispered. Again, she patted her cheeks with his handkerchief and then handed it back. "I'm okay now."

"You sure?"

"Yes, I've been keeping all this bottled up since coming to Gemini. Didn't want anyone to know—to suspect—"

"I know. I've been keeping a lot of stuff inside, too." He gave her hand a squeeze then withdrew and tucked the handkerchief back in his pocket.

Meg picked up her cup and sipped her tea. The hot liquid soothed. "Do you think there's a connection between what happened to Norrie and Johnny?"

"Sure looks that way. They both knew something someone didn't want discovered."

"If only we knew what it was."

Neither spoke. Meg idly gazed at the passing scene—cars hauling boats, bicycles with riders clad in spandex and helmets, and hikers laden with backpacks and bedrolls. An occasional horn tooted, and bits of conversation from the nearby tables floated along the air.

Finally, Eric spoke. "Something really worries me now."

His serious tone captured her attention. "What?"

"That Carl knows of your relationship to Johnny."

"I don't think he does." Meg bit her lip.

"I found out, didn't I?"

She spread her hands. "But you said you have connections."

Eric raised his eyebrows. "And a man like Carl doesn't?"

"Then don't you think he might know why you're here, too?"

"I'm not worried about me." He pointed at his chest. "I'm worried about you. You need to leave the island. This is dangerous business." He leaned forward, his eyes dark and serious. "Look, I'll take you to the ferry here on Orcas. When I return to Gemini, I'll tell them you got sick and had to go home."

"If Carl knows who I am, then will I be any safer at home? I talked to my friend who lives next door to Johnny, where I used to live, too, before the divorce." Meg shifted in her seat. "She said she saw a light in a second-story room. She thought I was there. But I was already on Gemini. I can't imagine who the intruder was or how they could have bypassed the security system."

"Okay, don't go home. Get on a plane and fly somewhere else. You must know someone you can stay with until this is solved."

"There's no one. Besides, I don't want to go anywhere." She lifted her chin. "So, I'm in danger. Why should you care?"

He threw up his hands. "I don't know. But I do. I don't want anything to happen to you. I'll take you to the ferry now."

Meg tightened her hand into a fist. "But I'll have left my belongings on Gemini."

"I'll pack them up and send them to you." He folded his arms. "Come on, don't give me any trouble. I want you out of the area. Out of danger."

Meg straightened her spine and propped her hands on her hips. "*You* want me out of here? You don't have anything to say about it. I have just as much right as you to be nosing around Gemini."

Eric set his jaw. "You need to leave."

"You can't make me leave." Meg raised her voice a notch. "Carl hired me, and he's the only one who can fire me. Besides, I want to stay. I *need* to stay."

Eric leaned back and studied her. "Why?"

Meg bit her lip. Should she bare more of her soul to Eric? Yet hadn't he opened a wound moments ago when he'd told her about Norrie?

She took a deep breath. "Okay, I'll tell you why. Johnny wanted us to be together again, but I said no. I'd heard he was seeing someone. I don't know who. But maybe if I'd agreed to let him come back, I wouldn't be mourning their deaths."

"You can't know that for sure. And, think about it this way." He tapped his forefinger on the tabletop. "If you'd been together, maybe you'd be dead as well."

"There's more...." Meg lowered her eyelids.

"Go on."

She twisted her fingers together in her lap and swallowed hard. "The night of the accident, I asked Johnny to pick up Alyssa from the hospital. I had a blind date a friend arranged. The date meant nothing, and I've never seen the man since. But I keep thinking, if only I had picked up Alyssa, instead of Johnny, she'd be alive today." Tears welled again. She squeezed her eyes shut to keep them from falling. She felt Eric's hand on her arm and found the subtle, warm pressure of his fingers comforting.

"I understand," he said simply.

She opened her eyes and met his gaze. Something passed between them, a brief moment of being exactly in sync with each other. Seizing on that, she said, "So, don't you see? If Johnny was set up, and I can help prove it, maybe then I'll be rid of the guilt. Maybe I'll sleep at night without nightmares. Maybe I'll find peace. That's why I must go back with you to Gemini."

The softness in Eric's eyes faded. He pulled his hand from her arm. "Out of the question. Too dangerous."

"I'm not afraid." On the contrary, the idea of facing danger sent blood rushing through her veins, making her feel more alive than she'd felt in months.

Several long moments passed, and then Eric cast her a sideways glance. "I suppose if we don't work together, you'll go off on your own."

Meg suppressed a smile. "There's a good chance I will, yes."

More seconds ticked by, and then he threw up his hands. "You win."

She blew out a relieved breath. "Partners, then?"

"Right—partners."

****

After they left the restaurant, they stopped at a nearby grocery. Eric grabbed a basket and pushed it down the aisles.

Meg selected wheat crackers, chocolate chip cookies, a brick of cheddar cheese, and a box of Earl Grey tea. In the produce section, she put a few apples into a plastic bag. "Aren't you buying anything?"

"Sure am." He steered them into the liquor aisle, where he grabbed a couple six packs of beer and set them in the cart.

She pressed her lips together and shook her head.

He shrugged. "So? You have your idea of what's good to have on hand, and I have mine."

They made their purchases and started back to the boat. Their talk today had changed their relationship. People they both cared about had died under mysterious circumstances. She believed what he'd told her. He spoke of Norrie and her death with deep and genuine emotion. He was as firm in his purpose as she was in hers.

Yes, she and Eric knew each other a lot better now. But, would their bond be strong enough to enable them to work together?

Chapter Ten

"Looks like a change in the weather," Eric remarked when they reached the boat.

Meg eyed the dark-bellied clouds and then the whitecaps dotting the water. A chill wind had sprung up, too, and she shivered and hugged her arms. "Maybe we should wait until it blows over.

Eric set the shopping bags on the boat's deck. "Gemini isn't far. We can make it okay. We'd better shove off, though, before the weather gets any worse."

Meg considered pressing her suggestion to wait but then changed her mind and kept quiet. The time was already late afternoon, and striking out now was preferable to making the trip after dark.

Or to staying the night on Orcas.

They stowed their purchases under the seat and put on their life jackets. Meg sat on the padded seat, and Eric took his place at the wheel. Once they were underway, he kept the boat's nose high in the air, hitting the waves broadside, which took them on a roller coaster ride from wave to trough and back to wave again.

Brushing wind-tossed hair from her eyes, Meg looked ahead to Gemini. Sitting on the horizon, with the mountain poking into the dark sky, the island appeared impossibly distant. She thought of her cottage, Wolf House, her cozy living room and kitchen, her bed in the loft, and longed to be there.

If she'd known the weather would take this turn, she never would have consented to today's trip. She'd lived in the northwest long enough to know sudden weather changes were the norm rather than the exception. But today, the weather had been the last thing on her mind. Instead, she'd focused on finding out about Eric.

Looking over her shoulder at Orcas, she saw the faint outline of a green-and-white ferry sailing away toward Seattle. Not even a storm such as this put the ferries out of service. For a moment, she wished she'd taken Eric's advice and let him deliver her to the ferry terminal. If she had, she'd be on the boat right now, settled in a well-protected area drinking hot coffee, hardly aware of the churning water and the strong wind.

Instead, she was here with Eric in this small boat, bouncing along toward an island where she'd established a new, though temporary, home. She turned and peered ahead.

A thick curtain of gray fog had fallen, and the island was no longer visible.

Meg licked her dry lips. She leaned toward him and yelled, "How will we find our way through the fog?"

He took a hand from the wheel long enough to point to the compass built into the dashboard. "No problem."

"And you know Gemini's compass heading?"

"Of course."

Of course, she mimicked after he had turned back to his steering. Was there anything he didn't know?

As if the threat of fog wasn't bad enough, rain

began to drum on the boat's fiberglass top. Gusts of wind swept the rain underneath. Meg clutched her jacket closer to her chest, but she was soon soaked anyway.

A large sailboat swept by, waves crashing over its bow. Two yachts followed, all headed for Orcas. No boats traveled in their direction. Apparently, they were the only ones with enough nerve—or stupidity—to venture outside sheltered waters.

Closer and closer crept the fog. Like a giant octopus, its tentacles reached out to capture them.

Another boat, much larger than theirs, appeared on their port side. Meg leaned forward. "Eric! There's another boat!"

Eric turned to look, but just then, the fog swallowed them, and the other boat disappeared.

"What if we run into someone?" Meg tightened her grip on her seat.

"Doubt it. Anything bigger than we are will have radar. Besides, not many boats are out."

Meg's heartbeat raced. "All it takes is one."

He shook his head and went back to his steering.

Presently, the drone of a boat's engine penetrated the fog. Meg tensed and cocked her head. Was this boat the same one she'd seen earlier, off the port side? Or was it a different craft? She glanced at Eric. He gave no notice of another boat, keeping his gaze focused on the waters directly ahead.

The motor's drone grew to a roar. "Eric! A boat's coming!"

"Yeah, I hear it."

"Do something!"

The other craft burst from the fog. About the same

size as *Wave Catcher*, the boat headed straight for them. Meg screamed and clutched the seat.

Eric jerked the wheel. *Wave Catcher* leaped forward, but not fast enough.

The other boat bore down, ready to hit them square on.

Her throat closed, and she braced herself for the collision.

Then, at the last possible second, the other boat swerved, narrowly missing them, and roared by.

A huge wall of water engulfed *Wave Catcher*. The boat rocked violently. The engine sputtered and then died.

Eric jammed his thumb against the starter button. The motor ground but failed to engage. Again and again he tried, but the engine remained stubbornly silent.

Intending to move farther under the protective roof, Meg struggled to her feet. At the same time, the boat plunged into a trough. She lost her footing on the slippery deck and slammed against the gunwale. Before she could grab onto anything, she tumbled over the side and into the water. The force of her landing plunged her below the surface. The sudden coldness shocked her senses.

She came up spitting water and flailing her arms. Even with the life jacket, she could barely keep her head above the churning water. Through her blurry vision, she glimpsed their boat a few yards away. She dog paddled frantically toward it, but the boat remained out of reach. Was Eric aware she'd gone over the side? The sound of the grinding engine indicated his determination to start the boat again. Still, he must have heard her scream.

But what if he hadn't? "Eric! Help!" She paddled harder.

The gulf between her and the boat continued to widen. Fear of being abandoned gripped her. Her throat tightened. This couldn't be happening. She'd fallen into a ghastly nightmare.

"Hang on, Meg! I'm coming!"

Yes! He'd seen her.

Eric drove an oar deep into the water, guiding the disabled boat toward her. When the gap was almost closed, he tossed the oar to the bottom of the boat and grabbed a life preserver. "Meg! Here!"

She reached out to catch the flying preserver. The ring fell short, hit the water with a splat, and bobbed on the waves. Okay, next time, she'd catch it.

Eric reeled in the preserver and threw it again.

Treading water, she strained to reach out—and missed. A groan escaped her lips.

The sound of a boat's motor filled the air. The same one that almost hit them? A knot formed in her stomach. *No, please, not that maniac again.*

The other boat burst from the fog. The bow was aimed directly at her.

The boat would mow her down. She was going to die.

Eric tossed the preserver.

The ring hit the tips of her fingers and then slid down over her hand. *Yes!* Her fingers were nearly frozen, but she managed to wrap her other hand around the rope and hang on.

The other boat swooped by, barely missing her.

Waves washed over her head, but she held on to her lifeline and kicked her feet while hand-over-hand,

Eric pulled her toward their boat. Any moment, she expected the other boat to return. The sound of an idling motor indicated the craft was still nearby.

Several times her grip on the preserver faltered, but she held on. Finally, a wave pushed her into the side of the boat. She reached up to grasp Eric's outstretched arms. They both grunted and groaned, and at last, she put her knee on the gunwale and tumbled aboard.

"Thank God!" He held her tight for a moment and then hustled her toward the cabin.

"Th-the other b-boat…"

"Never mind. Need to get you warm." He guided her down the steps and into the cabin. They passed the galley and then entered the bow of the boat. Sitting her on the bunk, he said in a no-nonsense tone, "Take off your clothes. All of them. I'll find a blanket."

Now wasn't the time for modesty. He was right. The water had been icy cold and hypothermia posed a danger. He helped her out of the cumbersome life jacket and then left her to do the rest while he rummaged in the storage area under the other bunk.

Meg's fingers were so cold she could barely make them work, and her teeth chattered so hard she feared they would break, but she managed to peel off her wet clothing.

Eric mumbled as he pawed through the storage locker. "Aha!" Snatching up a couple blankets, he tossed them onto the bed. "Here you go."

"T-thanks." She grasped a blanket and slung it around her shoulders.

He came to her side and wrapped her in the second blanket. Soon she was completely cocooned, and warmth seeped into her.

A boat's motor sounded in the distance.

Meg tensed. "The other boat. It's coming back."

Eric's lips thinned. "I'll get them this time." He headed toward the steps to the deck.

"Eric. No." How could they defend themselves in a broken-down boat?

Eric straightened his shoulders and stomped up the steps.

She heard him running along the deck. Judging by the roar of the motor, she knew the other boat still advanced.

The motor's roar diminished to a hum. She peered out the narrow window. A second boat bobbed in the water alongside them. Two figures stood on deck. Voices called out, "Yo, Eric! Meg!" Familiar voices. Burke? Jones? She heard Eric talking to them, but the wind blew away their words.

Finally, Eric clattered down the steps and stuck his head in the bow.

"Burke and Jones?" Meg asked.

He grinned. "Yep. They're gonna tow us in. You warming up?"

"I am. I'll be fine."

The men tied *Wave Catcher's* bow to the back of Jones and Burke's boat, and they were underway. Meg huddled in the bunk, relieved to be heading for Gemini at last. Still, she wondered about the sudden appearance of the two men. How had they known she and Eric were in trouble? Had they come across the other boat that attempted to run down *Wave Catcher*?

Another thought sent new chills down her spine. Maybe there was no other boat. Maybe, for some twisted reason, their attackers were also their rescuers.

****

"How're you doing?" Carl bent over Meg's bed and peered down.

Seeing the concern in his gaze, she managed a smile. "I'm okay."

"Warm enough?" Laureen tucked the quilt tighter around Meg. "I can get you another blanket."

"No, thanks, but I really appreciate you and Carl coming here to Wolf House to make sure I'm okay."

"'Course we would. Ya had us worried when we saw Eric helpin' you off the boat." Laureen poured coffee from a thermos into a porcelain mug and handed it to Meg. "Here's some hot coffee. Ya need to keep your insides warm."

Meg grasped the mug with both hands, letting the warmth seep into her skin. She took a sip. The rich brew tasted wonderful.

"Hypothermia doesn't take long in these cold waters." Carl straightened and shoved his hands into his slacks' pockets.

"I wasn't in the water long, thanks to Eric. Or in the boat afterward, thanks to Burke and Jones. Good thing they happened along." She slanted him a glance.

Carl's mouth tightened. "They didn't just happen. They were out looking for you. When the storm came up and I heard you hadn't returned, I told them to find you."

"I'm thankful for them, whatever the circumstances. And, I'm sorry Eric and I caused you so much trouble. We should've stayed on Orcas until the storm passed."

Carl made a dismissive wave, flashing his onyx ring. "Don't worry about it."

Meg sipped more coffee. "Did all your guests get home okay?"

"I haven't heard otherwise. They left well before the storm came up. Most were going to Seattle, but some were returning to vacation homes on neighboring islands. A few remained here."

"Oh?"

"Yes, Helen and Kent stayed. And Addie and Norm. They'll be working here for a while. Saves me making so many trips to Seattle."

"I see. Well, I'm sure I'll be back at work tomorrow." She held out her mug and accepted Laureen's refill. "Oh, did Eric tell you why we got in trouble?"

Carl frowned. "The other boat? Yes, he told me all about it."

"I don't know exactly what they were trying to do, capsize us, ram us, or just scare us. But their harassment sent me overboard."

He shrugged. "Probably kids lacking boating experience."

Meg shifted under the covers. "I wish I'd caught the name of the boat, or something to identify it. Then we could report them. But everything happened too fast."

"Best to let the matter go. You and Eric are safe. That's the important thing."

"I guess." Meg pressed her lips together. She hated to see whoever had caused their accident get away without being reported to the authorities.

"We'll let you rest now. Unless you need Laureen to stay?"

"I'll be fine by myself."

"Okay, but give a call if you want your supper brought here." He nodded to the phone on the bedside table.

"No, no. I want to come to the house for dinner."

"I'll have your wet clothes washed and dried by tomorrow," Laureen said.

"Thank you. I'd appreciate that." She watched them disappear down the stairs, thinking how kind and solicitous they both were. Surely, if anything bad or criminal was happening on Gemini, neither Carl nor Laureen was involved.

The front door opened and closed, and all was quiet. Meg finished her coffee and set the mug on the bedside table. A few minutes later, the door opened again. She tensed. Who could that be? Footsteps approached the stairs.

"Meg?" Eric called. "I brought your groceries. I'll put them away."

She smiled at his thoughtfulness. "Okay, thanks."

The sound of the refrigerator door slamming and cupboards opening and closing drifted up the stairs. Then he called, "I'm coming up." In no time at all, he reached the loft. He strode to her side and gazed down. "Hey."

"Hey, yourself." Remembering he'd seen her naked, Meg pulled up the quilt to her chin.

A smile tugged his lips.

Was he remembering, too?

Eric pulled up a straight chair beside the bed and sat. He leaned toward her.

Dangerously close. He was all clean and neat in fresh jeans and a blue, short-sleeved shirt. She caught a whiff of soap and aftershave.

"How're you doing?" He took a piece of paper from his shirt pocket and handed it to her.

"What's this?" She pulled a hand from under the quilt and took the paper.

He put a finger to his lips and shook his head.

She studied the message. *Be careful what you say. Your cottage may be bugged. Mine is.*

Raising her gaze to his, she widened her eyes. "Uh, I'm doing okay."

He took back the paper. "I'm really sorry about what happened."

"My falling overboard wasn't your fault. If the other boat hadn't come along, we'd have been fine."

Smiling, he nodded. "I agree. Thanks for the vote of confidence."

"Hey, you pulled me out of the water."

"I'd sure like to know the identity of the boat that almost ran us down."

"Carl said it was probably inexperienced kids." She shook her head. She wanted to tell him her suspicion about Burke and Jones being both their tormentors and their rescuers. But, in case her cottage was bugged, she'd save her comments until later.

Eric raised a skeptical eyebrow, but said smoothly, "He's probably right." He took a pencil from his shirt pocket and wrote something on the paper. He showed it to her: *Maybe.*

She met his gaze and nodded.

"Do you need anything?" He tucked the paper and pencil back into his shirt pocket.

"No, I'm all taken care of. Laureen brought me coffee. And water." She laughed. "Although I've seen enough of *that* to last a while."

He shifted in the chair. "Okay, then. Oh, how about dinner?"

"I'll go to the house. Definitely."

"I'll come by for you." He stood and glanced around. "Storm's over, but the air's cool. Dress warm."

His concern touched her. "I'll be sure to wear a jacket."

"Good. Wouldn't want you catching cold. Not after all my work to warm you up." He grinned.

With that, he was gone.

Chapter Eleven

"And then the sucker swerved and darn near took the end off of my boat. Just like what happened to you two today." Norm waved his fork at Meg and Eric.

"I swear, traffic is as bad on the water as on the highways," Addie chimed in. "Reckless drivers everywhere."

Eric helped himself to more mashed potatoes and then passed the dish to Norm. "You got that right, Addie."

Meg nodded her agreement and took another bite of Laureen's pot roast. Hers and Eric's adventure had triggered the memories of Carl and his guests, and nearly everyone at the dinner table had a story of a boating accident or near-accident. Norm's tale, about fishing alone off the shores of California, was the most harrowing so far. His recitation was also the longest speech she'd heard from him since he arrived. He usually let his wife do the talking.

Lester looked around the table. "I've got one that happened to my girlfriend, in Canada."

"Ah, yes." Addie rolled her eyes. "The mysterious girlfriend in Canada."

Lester gave her a smirk. "She was out fishing with her father, and the fog came in, and they almost ran into a cruise ship."

"That could be a problem," Carl said dryly, from

his place at the head of the table. He turned to Helen, sitting at his right, "What about you?"

She shook her head and absently smoothed the collar of her pink blouse. "I'm not much of a boater. Just ask Kent." She nodded to where he sat across the table.

Kent sipped his wine and set down the glass. "True enough. You should have seen her on the ferry to Orcas. Just like a little kid, she kept asking me, 'Are we there yet?'"

After everyone finished laughing, Carl gazed around the table and rubbed his hands together. "Now, let's talk about the potlatch we'll have here in a couple weeks."

"I've read about those." Meg leaned in their host's direction. "It's a big party one Northwest Indian tribe gave for another tribe, isn't it?"

Carl nodded. "Right. Usually, an important occasion was involved, like an anniversary or a birthday. The chief hosting the party presented gifts to the other tribe. When the second chief reciprocated with his own party, he attempted to outdo the gifts of the first chief."

"A game of 'can you top this?'" Lester put in. "Human nature never changes much, does it?"

"Now, Les." Addie waggled a finger. "Let Carl have his fun. Maybe your girlfriend can come," she added with a sly look.

"Which tribes will be in your potlatch?" Meg touched her napkin to her lips.

"Mine's a variation on the theme," Carl said. "My friends and I will be the inviting tribe, with me as chief, of course." He straightened and thumbed his chest.

"And, we're inviting the Nootlinga. I've been working with them for several years and know them pretty well."

"Is Jones Nootlinga?" Eric asked.

"As a matter of fact, he is. I met him on the res." Carl frowned and quirked an eyebrow. "You familiar with the Noots, Eric?"

Meg held her breath. Surely, Eric wouldn't talk about Norrie.

Eric shrugged. "I gamble at the casino on the res now and then. I just wondered if Jones would be part of your potlatch."

Carl's smile chased away his frown. "Yes, he and Burke have much to do, both beforehand and during."

"So, are you planning to give lots of gifts?" Meg relaxed, now the matter of Jones had been settled.

"Or course, he is." Kent stabbed his fork into a piece of steak. "Carl's famous for his potlatches, just like some of the Indian chiefs of the past."

"Too bad you weren't around back then." Helen smiled at Carl. "You'd be king of the potlatches."

"No doubt I would have been. Providing I had the backing of my Fortune Industries." Carl grinned while polite laughter rippled around the table. "And, yes, Meg, I am giving gifts. Most of them will be reproductions of the trinkets I've collected, but I have one special gift. A surprise none of you—no, not even you, Addie, who knows *everything* about *everybody*—will discover until then."

Addie widened her eyes. "Ooooh, now I'm really curious."

"My favorite part of the potlatch is the food," Norm acknowledged, taking another bite of pot roast.

Addie poked his large belly with her forefinger. "No surprise there, Norm, darling."

Carl nodded and sipped his wine. "Good food, yes. Of course, we'll have salmon, cooked over open pits on alder wood planks, roasted corn, and potatoes."

"Sounds like fun." Meg's enthusiasm grew.

"It will be, but we have a lot of work to do until then. Right, crew?" Eyebrow raised, he looked around the table.

Helen, Norm, Kent, and Lester all nodded obediently.

"I'm the only one who'll have any free time," Addie said. "But I'm sure I can find something to do.

Laureen bustled in with a tray of cheesecake slices, each with a different topping. When her turn came to choose, Meg gazed in awe at the variety. "Did you make these?"

"I wish. But, no, Jones and Burke bought them at the bakery on Orcas."

An internal alarm went off. Avoiding looking at Eric, she focused on the desserts. "They were on Orcas? Today?"

"Uh huh. On an errand for Carl. So, I asked them could they do me a favor. Good thing they were around to rescue you and Eric, huh?"

"Right." Meg chose a slice topped with cherries. As she ate, she mulled over Laureen's news about Burke and Jones. So, they'd been on Orcas today, too. Carl told her he sent them to look for her and Eric in the storm. Had they made their trip to Orcas, returned to Gemini, and then been sent? Or had Carl cooked up an errand, so they could keep an eye on her and Eric the entire time?

****

After dinner, with the storm over and the sky clear once again, Carl suggested they adjourn to poolside for drinks. At first, Meg warmed to the idea, but when she saw Helen and Eric step outside together, she changed her mind. "If you don't mind, Carl, I'll return to my cottage. I could use the extra rest."

He squeezed her shoulder. "Of course. You've been through an ordeal today. Do you need anything?"

"No. I'll be fine, thanks." Meg turned toward the path.

Eric broke away from Helen and approached Meg. "I'll walk with you."

"No need. I'd rather go alone."

Helen joined them. "Of course, you should see Meg to her cottage, Eric. You're such a gentleman. And, we're so glad you're all right, Meg, dear."

At Helen's honeyed tones, Meg inwardly cringed. What was the woman's game, anyway?

Helen laid a hand on Eric's arm. "We'll have a drink together when you come back."

"Ah, sure, Helen. See you later."

"I'll look for you." She gave him a bright smile and turned to rejoin the others, who were settling into chairs and giving their drink orders to Burke.

Eric fell into step beside Meg on the path leading to the cottages.

"You don't have to come with me," she said again. "Stay and have a drink with Helen."

"I want to come with you." He put his mouth close to her ear. "I want to check for bugs."

"Oh, right. Good idea."

A few minutes later, Meg watched Eric scan her

living room and kitchen with his bug sweeper, as he called the electronic device small enough to fit in the palm of his hand. The radio on the kitchen counter played soft rock music from the station he selected before beginning his search.

"I could use something to drink," he said over his shoulder.

"All I have are tea or coffee."

"Coffee's fine."

She opened the cupboard containing the tin of coffee. "If you'd stayed with the others, you'd be enjoying Carl's fancy after-dinner liqueur."

"This is more important. I wanted to run a sweep this afternoon, after Carl and Laureen left, but I didn't want to risk them catching me. And, I wanted you to see what I find, if anything."

Eric's hunt revealed three electronic bugs—one in the phone, one behind the seascape hanging on the living room wall, and the other behind a picture of seagulls in the loft. "Your bugs are in the same place as mine." He turned off the device and stuck it in his shirt pocket. "And from now on, when we're discussing stuff we don't want others to hear, we turn that on." He pointed to the radio.

She frowned as she poured their coffee. "Can't you take them out? I don't like my privacy being invaded."

He raised an eyebrow. "What's going on in your cottage that's so private?"

She rolled her eyes. "You know what I mean."

"Okay, but no, we're leaving them just where they are." He picked up his mug.

Meg paced the kitchen while sipping her coffee. "Why would Carl bug his guest cottages?"

"Maybe he's just nosy and likes to listen in on people." Eric leaned one hip against the counter. "Then again, maybe the bugs aren't Carl's doing."

"Maybe not." Meg stopped pacing. "What about the museum? Is it bugged, too?"

"Not that I could discover."

"You've already checked it out?" Surprise laced her voice. "Where was I?"

He set down his mug and folded his arms. "I went out early the first morning and looked around before you arrived."

She narrowed her eyes. "Where'd you learn how to check for bugs, anyway? Who are you?"

"What do you mean? You know who I am." He picked up his mug and held it out. "How 'bout a refill?"

Okay, she'd let her questions go—for now. But his evasiveness raised a warning flag. Should she place her trust in him, after all? Yet, what choice had she? She went to the stove, but before picking up the coffee pot, she turned to him again. "Sure you want more coffee? You're, ah, free to go."

He chuckled. "Still trying to get rid of me. Such hospitality." Then he sobered. "Seriously, Meg, if you want to rest, I'll leave. But if you have the energy, we could spend a few minutes talking about where we go from here."

"I'm sorry." Meg ran a hand over her forehead. "I do appreciate the bug search. And, you're right—we should talk." She picked up the coffee pot, refilled their cups, and led the way to the living room.

She sat on the sofa, expecting him to take the chair opposite. Instead, he settled beside her. Another warning flag went up. She kept her back rigid, her elbow on the armrest. "So, what's next on our agenda?"

Eric rested his ankle on his knee. "We return to work in the museum."

"How can we discover anything if we're stuck out there all day?" Meg wrinkled her nose.

"We have to maintain appearances. We'll watch for opportunities to look around. After dark is the best time to take a closer look at the mountain."

Meg's stomach tightened. "And risk running into Burke and Jones?"

He leaned close and patted her hand. "I'll protect you."

"The way you protected Norrie?" Meg blurted then gasped. "Oh, I-I'm so sorry." She bit her lip. "That was uncalled for." Shame flushed her cheeks. Why hadn't she thought before she spoke?

Eric rested his elbows on his knees and stared at the floor. "Yeah, well, that's why I'm here, isn't it? To make up for failing Norrie."

"We're both doing penance," she reminded him. "I made my mistakes, too. But I never should have said what I did. My remark was cruel, and I'm really, really sorry." She laid a hand on his arm.

He straightened and placed his hand over hers. "Apology accepted. Today has been tough for both of us."

She forced a mirthless laugh. "You've got that right. Maybe I should have taken your advice and gone home." Unexpected tears burned her eyes.

He cupped her chin and gazed into her eyes. "Hey, hey, don't cry. You're still here, and we're gonna solve this problem, I promise you."

She swallowed against a tight throat. "I hope so.

But shouldn't you be getting back to the party? Helen's waiting."

He smoothed a lock of hair from her forehead. His hand lingered, caressing her skin. "Look, I will meet her, because maybe she knows something that will help us. But she can wait. Right now, I'd rather be here…with you."

They stared at each other. The air around them stilled. His eyes closed and his lips parted.

She caught his scent, his maleness mixed with whiskey and coffee. His hot breath brushed her cheek. Powerless to resist, she leaned toward him.

A low moan escaped his lips, and then his mouth covered hers. The kiss was soft, and sweet. He moved closer still and gathered her into his arms.

With a sigh, she wrapped her arms around his neck and gave herself to the kiss.

"I want you," he murmured when at last he drew away.

His words sent heat coursing through her body.

"Say you want me, too. I know you do. Say it."

"I…I can't.

He drew back and gazed through narrowed eyes. "Why not?"

She touched her lips, struggling with her jumbled emotions. Yes, she did want him. Desperately. But she wouldn't give in to her desire. Too scary. Way too scary. "I'm not interested in a relationship," she said, her tone more stiff than she'd intended.

His eyelids flickered. "Who said anything about a relationship?"

"Oh, silly me. Of course, a man like you wouldn't be interested in something so mundane."

Eric stiffened. "My, what big words you use. I'm impressed."

The mood of a few seconds ago vanished like smoke in the wind. She scooted to the edge of the sofa. "I really am tired. Would you mind leaving now?"

"Yeah, I mind." His voice was husky again. "But I'm on my way." He didn't move. Seconds drifted by. Finally, he stood and picked up their empty mugs.

She put out a hand. "Don't bother. I'll clean up."

"Already done," he said over his shoulder as he headed for the kitchen. When he finished, he returned to the living room and stood gazing down at her. "Sure you're gonna be okay?"

She hated the caring in his voice and wished he'd be flippant again instead. With both hands, she made shooing motions. "Go already."

He wheeled and strode to the door. Then he opened it and walked out.

"Have fun with Helen," she called just before the door slammed shut.

Chapter Twelve

Sitting at her desk in the museum workroom the next morning, Meg glanced at Eric. He was bent over his worktable, examining several carved wooden bowls. They'd been at work for an hour now, and she kept waiting to hear about his meeting last night with Helen. But he hadn't mentioned it. She considered asking, squelched the idea, and buried herself in her data entries.

Still, the matter nagged her, and finally, when they were eating lunch on the patio, she could no longer contain her curiosity. "So, did you find out anything useful from Helen last night?" She kept her tone casual.

Eric snorted. "That turned out to be a big nothing."

"Oh, really?"

"Carl said she went to her cottage. Addie was reading, and the guys were playing poker." He helped himself to another ham sandwich. "I sat in on a couple hands and then went back to my place."

She wanted to ask if he'd stopped by Helen's cottage, because maybe her goal had been to lure him there. Instead, she bit back the words. Hadn't she promised herself, no more petty jealousy?

"I didn't stop by Helen's cottage, if you're wondering."

Meg picked at her potato salad. "If I am, it's only because I'm interested in knowing if you learned anything from her that will help us."

"Right. Well, the answer is, not yet. But maybe next time."

****

After dinner that evening, Meg purposely kept a distance from Eric. If he meant to hook up with Helen, for whatever purpose, she wouldn't interfere.

Outside, Norm and Addie were on their way to the pool for an after-dinner swim. "Oh, there you are." Addie waved to Meg. "I thought you were with Eric." She pressed a finger to her lips. "Oh, wait, that was Helen. They went off somewhere together." She gave Meg a sly look.

"Well, good for them." Meg hoped Addie got the message that she couldn't care less what Eric did or with whom.

Sounds of laughter and the clinking of glasses floated from the softly illuminated patio, but Meg was not in the mood for socializing. She bypassed the party and headed down the path to Wolf House. She looked forward to relaxing with a cup of hot tea and dipping into the snacks she'd bought on the trip to Orcas.

At her cottage, Meg took her cup of tea and a plate of cookies to the sofa and settled back against the cushions. A while later, she'd no more than put her empty teacup and plate in the sink than a knock sounded on the front door. She went to the window and peeked out.

Eric stood on the doorstep.

Remembering what had happened the previous evening when she'd let him into her cottage, Meg hesitated to answer the door.

He knocked again. "Meg. I know you're in there.

Open up."

Meg sighed. She'd better respond before someone came by and witnessed his noisy performance. Gritting her teeth, she opened the door a crack and peered out.

"Where've you been all evening?" he asked.

"Just hanging out here. According to Addie, you were occupied with Helen."

Eric frowned. "Addie's a busybody. But, hey, the night's still young. How about a walk on the beach?"

Go for a walk? Meg hesitated. But a walk would be better than letting him inside and risking another evening like the previous one. "Okay, let me grab a jacket." Tonight would be all business, she vowed, as she slipped into a windbreaker. No fooling around.

They left the cottages behind and followed a path through the woods. Just in case he decided to hold her hand, she tucked both into her jacket pockets. He kept his distance, too, staying well on his side of the path.

"Do you have a new plan?" she asked as they strolled along. A soft breeze rustled the leaves of the bushes lining the walk, and the air smelled fresh and clean.

He put a finger to his lips. "No talk yet. The woods might have ears. We'll wait until we get to the openness of the shore."

At the beach, the sand and the water sparkled under a rising moon. But when she glanced inland, she saw the shadows were long and dark, and the mountain loomed over them like an ever-watchful giant.

Eric pointed to a pile of logs at the high tide line. "We're not likely to be heard here, so let's sit."

"All right. For a little while."

"What's the rush? Got a hot date?"

His teasing tone grated on her nerves. "No, I just want to go back soon."

"Talk first."

She followed him to the logs where he made a sweeping motion with one hand. "Pick your spot."

"Doesn't really matter," she grumbled, and perched on the nearest log.

He sat beside her, picked up a stick, and poked at the sand.

Meg clasped her hands in her lap and stared at the water. The moon's pearly light cut a swath from horizon to shore. A few spindly-legged birds played in the froth of breaking waves and then took flight, disappearing into the twilight.

After a few minutes, Eric tossed away the stick and cleared his throat. "Meg, about last night…"

Meg stiffened. "I'd like to forget last night."

"Would you? Would you, really?"

"Yes, wouldn't you?"

He lifted one shoulder. "It happened."

"It won't happen again."

"Why not? You said you were over your husband. Is there someone else?"

She ran a hand across her forehead, sorting out her jumbled emotions. "No, there hasn't been anyone since Johnny. But I'm still grieving…my d-daughter…" Her throat choked up.

Eric put his arm around her shoulders. "I know what you're experiencing, believe me. Norrie was like a kid sister to me."

"That's just it. We're here to find out what happened to Norrie, and to Johnny and Alyssa. No sense complicating things by us getting involved."

Long moments passed, and she thought she'd had the last word.

"I hear you." He finally spoke in a low tone. "And you're right. Absolutely right. We're together only because we have a common goal. We'd better stick to that."

****

Meg lay in bed, unable to banish Eric from her thoughts. She'd told herself over and over that putting a stop to any personal involvement was the right decision. She'd only be using him to chase away her loneliness and grief, which was wrong.

True, she now saw another, nicer, side to him than the arrogance that put her off when they first met. He seemed capable of deep feelings, at least for Norrie.

So what? Becoming involved was a still bad idea. Chance had thrown them together. When they found the answers to their questions, they would end their association.

But, deep down, she knew her fear was the real reason for backing off tonight. She'd loved Johnny with all her heart. Watching their relationship deteriorate tore her apart. They hurt each other deeply. Worse, they hurt Aly, too.

Counselors told her Johnny's drinking wasn't her fault, but, still, she couldn't stop blaming herself. What had she done wrong? Why wasn't he happy? Why did he need to drink?

Tears filled Meg's eyes. She rolled over and let the tears soak into the pillow. No, she wasn't ready for a relationship, not even a casual one.

****

Eric sat on his sofa, staring at the melting ice in his

glass, all that was left of his Scotch-and-water. He'd needed something to cool him down after being with Meg. Not that the alcohol did much good. He was still wired. So much for his resolution to not get involved. He'd been successful denying the sparks flaring between them, but tonight his defenses hadn't worked.

But, hey, she turned him down. She was smarter than he was. Leaning his head against the cushions, he exhaled. He wished she'd taken his advice and returned to Seattle.

But she hadn't. Still, he needed to keep his mind on track. Which reminded him of the list of names he'd given Nick. He took out his cell phone and checked his messages. Sure enough, he had one from Nick. Man, the agent was fast. And thorough, too. He'd managed to find out something about every name on the list.

Eric studied the information, committing the facts to memory. Then he deleted the message. He idly tapped the phone's case with his forefinger. The next item on his agenda was to investigate the mountain.

****

On Wednesday morning at breakfast, Carl announced a short cruise aboard his yacht was scheduled for that afternoon. "We've been working hard for the past couple of days," he said, rubbing his hands together. "Time for a break. Everyone be at the dock at two p.m."

After her harrowing experience in the motorboat, Meg looked forward to a leisurely cruise aboard Carl's yacht. And maybe viewing the mountain from a new perspective would yield new information.

But later, in the museum workroom, Eric left his workbench and approached her desk. "We're not going to Carl's party."

His authoritative tone caught her attention. She stopped typing and looked up. "Why not?"

"We'll be checking out the mountain instead."

Ah, that might be better than what they could discover from aboard the yacht. Meg put her hands in her lap and gave him her full attention. "Sounds good. But what if Jones and Burke catch us?"

Shaking his head, Eric waved a hand. "They're Carl's crew and will be on the cruise. No one will catch us. The opportunity is perfect."

"How can we skip the party? You know how bossy Carl is about everyone following his plans."

"Good point." He stroked his chin. "But here's a way. We go aboard, along with everyone else. Then, just before they cast off, we go ashore."

Meg picked up her stack of cards and absently thumbed through them. "Won't somebody see us?"

"We'll say we forgot our cameras. We'll be gone so long they'll have to leave without us."

Meg chewed her bottom lip. "I don't know....Wouldn't both of us forgetting our cameras sound kind of phony?"

"Okay, we'll think of something else for you." Eric gazed at the ceiling.

"The whole plan sounds risky."

He turned to her and spread his hands. "Fine. If you don't want to come along, I'll go by myself. That option would probably be better, anyway." Giving a shrug, he strode back to his workbench.

She stared at his retreating back. "Oh, no, you're not getting rid of me so easily. Of course, I want to go. I'll figure out something."

****

At the appointed hour, Meg and Eric joined the others at the dock and boarded Carl's seventy-foot yacht, *The Lady Fortune*. Carl led them directly to the salon's bar for cocktails. Once everyone was served, he insisted on taking Meg and Eric on a tour. Under other circumstances, Meg would have been a willing, even eager, guest, but today's goal to ditch the cruise and remain on the island kept her nerves taut.

"...four cabins, a galley, and a Jacuzzi topside." Carl beamed like a proud father. "And, of course, you've noticed my Northwest Indian artwork." He pointed to the ceremonial masks hanging beside the mirror over the bar. "All replicas, of course. I wouldn't risk my originals here."

Eric studied the masks. "And very good copies they are. I bet not many of your guests know the difference. By the way, where are we off to today?"

"A short jaunt to Orcas. Everyone's been there, of course, but the scenery never fails to please."

Shaking his head, Eric snapped his fingers. "Speaking of scenery, I forgot my camera."

"No problem. I keep disposables on hand for that very reason." Carl nodded to a pile of small cameras on a nearby table.

"Disposables..." Eric knit his brow. "No offense, Carl, but I promised to email some pics to my sister and her kids. I really need my own camera. I'll only take a few minutes to run back to the cottage and get it."

Carl looked at his wristwatch. "Forget it. We're leaving in five minutes. Can't wait any longer. Our schedule. The tides."

"I'll hurry." Eric crossed to the bar and set down

his beer bottle.

Helen swiveled on her bar stool. "Did I hear you say you're leaving?"

"Just to get my camera. Back in a flash."

"Wait—" Carl put out a hand.

Eric sprinted toward the door.

"I'll go with him." Meg set her wine glass on the bar. Leaving Carl with his jaw hanging open, she hurried after Eric.

At the door to the deck, Addie stepped in front of her. "Have you seen the cabins yet?"

Meg tensed. "No, I haven't, but—"

Addie adjusted the yellow scarf holding back her hair. "I'll give you a tour. They are positively gorgeous. All teakwood and fancy bedspreads and low lights. Very romantic."

"Yes, I'm sure they are." Meg craned her neck to see around Addie and spotted Eric stepping off the gangplank onto the dock. "But I need to help Eric. I'll be back in a few minutes. Then I'll let you show me around. I promise."

Addie tapped a forefinger against her wristwatch. "We're casting off soon."

"I know. We'll be back in time. Don't worry." Meg brushed past her and out the door. She ran to the railing and looked down the length of the dock. She expected to see Eric waiting for her, but he was nowhere in sight. Meg fumed. He could've waited to make sure she was able to escape, too. She hurried to the gangplank.

Jones stood guard, feet spread apart, arms crossed over his chest.

"I need to go with Eric...cameras," she told him.

The tall man shook his head. "The yacht is about to

shove off."

"We'll make it back in time." She ducked around him, ran down the gangplank, and jumped onto the dock. But a few steps later, when she leaped off the dock, she lost her balance, and her right foot twisted in the soft sand. Pain shot through her ankle, and with a gasp, she fell to her knees. Catching her breath took a couple moments. Then, pushing up with her hands, she staggered to her feet.

Meg limped up the embankment, wincing at every step. She was panting when she reached the top. Paths forked off to the main house, to the other docks, to the museum, and to the forbidden side of the island.

Eric had vanished. Except for the wind soughing in the trees, all was silent. Which path, if any, had he taken? Darn him, anyway. Why hadn't he waited?

Movement of the bushes up ahead caught her attention. The bushes parted, and Eric stepped onto the path.

She waved her arms and staggered toward him. "There you are. I thought you'd abandoned me."

"No, just getting a head start." His gaze moved to her right leg. "Are you limping?"

"Maybe a little. When I jumped off the dock, I stumbled and hurt my ankle."

Eric hurried to her side. He knelt and probed her ankle, pressing gently against the bones. "Doesn't appear to be broken."

Despite his soft touch, Meg winced. "Of course not. I knew that."

He looked up. "Sprained, then."

The concern in his eyes touched her, but she didn't want to be left behind. She shook her head. "Not even sprained."

Eric stood. "Okay, but you're obviously in pain. You'd better stay off the ankle and stick around here."

Uh oh, just what she'd feared. She folded her arms and shook her head. "No, I'm going with you."

"Meg..."

Before he could say any more, she summoned all her energy to exclaim, "I'm going!"

They glared at each other. Finally, he held out his hand. "Come on, then. Time's wasting."

Chapter Thirteen

Aided by a sturdy branch Eric had found, Meg followed him along the path leading to the mountain. Her ankle hurt, but walking was not as difficult as she'd feared. Overgrown with weeds and hanging branches, the route led them deeper into the island's interior. Eventually, they came upon a clearing where a mini tractor and backhoe like they'd seen at the museum were parked. Piles of brush and tree limbs littered the area.

"Looks like Carl is developing this part of the island," Meg said. "And keeping us away isn't just an excuse."

"Maybe not. But this message is pretty clear." Eric pointed to a wooden barricade with a boldly scrawled *Keep Out*.

Meg's shoulders drooped. "Now what?"

Eric approached the barricade. "I'll have no problem getting over, but you—"

Meg limped forward to join him. "If you give me a leg up, and if I'm careful of my ankle, I'm sure I can climb over. Then you can follow."

Glancing back and forth from her to the barrier, Eric finally nodded. "Okay, but be careful. I don't want any more injuries."

A few minutes later, they both stood on the other side of the barrier. Meg wanted to say, *See, I told you so*, but this was not the time to claim superiority. Instead, she brushed twigs and leaves from her hair and studied their surroundings. They were much closer to the mountain now. Like a dark giant, the peak loomed. Shrubs and rock outcroppings covered the lower slopes. Farther up grew small trees, and higher yet the taller, more substantial pine and fir. A satellite dish peeked above the trees. "What are we looking for?" Meg continued to gaze at the mountain.

"If the mountain is a hiding place for something—drugs, maybe—then an entrance must be somewhere. We'll see if we can find it."

They picked up sturdy sticks to poke and prod at the base of the mountain. They dug into the earth, sending mini landslides of dirt and small rocks cascading down the side. They pushed away branches and bushes, and then rolled away rocks. They found nothing.

Finally, Eric tossed down his stick and huffed out a breath. "We need to get back."

Meg ran a hand over her forehead. "I need to rest a minute first." She sank to the ground, leaned against the mountain, and propped her throbbing ankle on a log. Something solid pressed against her back, something neither earth nor bushes. She turned and pulled away enough foliage to reveal a large wooden plank. Her breath caught. "Eric, I've found something."

Eric ran to her side and joined her in tugging away the branches covering the plank. "I bet it's a door."

"If we can uncover more and figure out how to get in…" Meg added a handful of foliage to the pile they'd created.

In the distance, a boat's horn echoed.

Eric straightened and extended his hand. "No time now. That's Carl's yacht. We need to cover this back up and get out of here."

****

Twenty minutes later, on the patio at the main house, Meg lay on a chaise lounge, a cushion elevating her injured ankle.

Eric sat in a chair reading a newspaper. He'd found a towel and some ice at the portable bar and fashioned a makeshift wrap for her injury. He'd even had time to pour them drinks.

Meg gratefully sipped her white wine, a refreshing treat after their trek through the woods.

The sound of approaching golf carts broke the silence.

"Here they come." Certain Carl would be angry because they missed the cruise, Meg braced herself for a confrontation.

The first cart, driven by Burke, rumbled into view. Carl, Helen, Lester, and Kent alighted and walked toward them.

"There you are," Helen called out. "We wondered what happened."

Carl planted his hands on his hips and frowned at Eric. "I thought you said you'd only take a few minutes to get your camera?"

"Right." Eric folded the newspaper and laid it on a glass-top table. "But then Meg hurt her ankle."

Carl's probing gaze swung to Meg. "How did that happen?"

Meg winced as she adjusted her ankle wrap. "When I jumped off the dock, I fell and twisted my ankle."

140

Eric nodded. "She had trouble walking, and I needed to stay with her."

"So you spent the entire time here?" Helen's wave took in the patio.

Glancing around, Eric shrugged. "More or less."

Stroking his beard, Kent ambled to Meg and peered at her injured ankle. "Are you sure no bones are broken? Maybe you should see a doctor."

Meg made a dismissive wave. "Heavens, no. I don't think the ankle's even sprained. The ice is a precaution. I'll be all right by tomorrow."

"Maybe not," Lester chimed in. "I fell down the steps at my apartment and was outa commission for a coupla weeks."

With a smile, Eric turned to Helen. "How was the boat trip?"

Helen beamed. "Wonderful." She sat beside him and chattered about docking at Eastsound, visiting the "cutest little shops," and having drinks at an outdoor restaurant. All accompanied by gestures and tosses of her hair.

Meg inwardly rolled her eyes.

Jones drove up with Norm, Addie, and Laureen in his cart.

Addie jumped from the cart and rushed to the patio. "You should've let me give you a tour," she said to Meg when she heard the story. "Then you wouldn't have hurt yourself." She pointed to the glass in Meg's hand. "Is that wine?"

"Uh huh. A very nice Chardonnay." Meg held up her glass and sipped.

Eric turned to Carl. "Didn't think you'd mind us helping ourselves to the bar."

"Not at all." Carl rubbed his hands together and looked at the others. "Would anyone else like a drink?"

Addie tucked a lock of hair under her scarf. "I'll have a gin and tonic. How about you, Norm?"

Norm patted his potbelly. "I could do with a whiskey and soda."

The others chimed in with their requests.

Burke stepped behind the bar, and the sounds of ice clinking into glasses blended with the conversation.

Meg settled back to relax and finish her wine. But then she noticed Carl casting a frown first in Eric's and then in her direction, a frown that told her maybe he wasn't buying their story, after all.

****

After a dinner of poached halibut, baked potatoes, and roasted corn, Carl suggested the group return to the patio for drinks.

On the way, Meg pulled him aside and begged off, asking if someone could drive her to her cottage. Her ankle hurt, and she didn't want to risk walking any more than necessary.

He readily agreed and summoned Burke.

Meg did not relish the company of the burly giant, but reasoned if not Burke, her escort would have been Jones.

They started off, with Meg sitting in the cart's back seat. A rising moon peeped between the trees, bathing the path in a silver light, but not even the beautiful night could elevate her mood.

Burke glanced over his shoulder. "Too bad you fell off the dock."

Meg sighed. She'd hoped to make the trip in silence. "I didn't fall. When I jumped down, I lost my balance and twisted my ankle."

Burke steered the cart around a bend. "Carl wanted y'all on the cruise today. He don't like it when his orders are disobeyed."

In no mood to hear any more about Carl and his orders, Meg gritted her teeth. "I had an accident. Missing the boat trip was unavoidable."

"You 'n Eric spent all the time on the patio?"

He's the second one to ask that. "Why do you ask?"

He shot her another glance. "Security's my job. You get into trouble, I get into trouble."

She leaned forward and gripped the back of his seat. "But you were on the yacht. How could you be in two places at once? If Carl wanted you to guard the island, he should have left you here."

His shoulders hunched. "Still my responsibility."

Meg sighed again and sat back. No use continuing the argument when Burke had to have the last word. They finally reached her cottage. Glancing at the totem pole wolf's leer, Meg shivered and hugged her arms. Still, she was glad to be at her home-away-from-home.

Burke ground the cart to a halt. He turned, his eyes flat in the deepening twilight. "Need some help gettin' out?"

Meg scooted to the edge of the seat. "No, thanks. I can manage." The thought of him touching her, even to help, gave her the creeps. Holding on to the metal railing, she carefully alighted.

"Best to obey the rules around here," Burke warned.

"Yes, I think you've made that clear."

****

Meg sat on her sofa, with her leg propped on a footstool. On her lap lay one of her reference books, *Northwest Indian Masks and Ceremonial Costumes*. She'd given up reading and had let the book fall shut.

A knock on her door jolted her from her half-asleep state. She glanced at her wristwatch. Nine o'clock. Who could be calling at this hour? Burke, checking up on her?

Meg limped to the window and peered discreetly through the blinds.

Eric.

Her stomach clenched. She had expected he would seek her out sometime, but not tonight. She didn't want to deal with him. Her ankle hurt, and fatigue had drained her.

Again he knocked on the door. "I know you're in there, Meg, so open up."

Pursing her lips, she unlocked and opened the door a crack. Before she could tell him to go away, he pushed open the door and slid inside.

Meg glared. "I didn't invite you in."

He stopped in the middle of the living room and propped both hands on his hips. "I thought you might need some help—because of your ankle."

"Nothing you can do. I'll be fine." She made a dismissive wave.

"Yeah, I saw you limp off with Burke. You were hurting."

"No concern of yours."

"How 'bout a cup of coffee? And some music?" He pointed to the bugged seascape on the wall before crossing to the counter and turning on the portable radio. "What do you like? Classical? Rock?"

She shrugged. "Whatever. But if you want coffee, you'll have to make it."

"Sure. You sit. Take a load off your ankle." He rolled the radio's dial, stopping on a soft rock station. "You left the party early," he said, rounding the counter into the kitchen and opening cupboards.

Meg returned to the sofa. "Coffee's in the cupboard to the left. Okay, my ankle is bothering me. Besides, you and Helen were having a good time. I didn't think you'd miss me."

Understanding lighted his eyes. "Ah, so that's it. A little jealous, are we?"

She bit her lip, wishing she could take back the words. What was the matter with her? Evidently, pain and fatigue had weakened her self-control. She folded her arms and stuck her nose in the air. "Not in the least."

"Helen may be a part of whatever's happening here. I want to learn all I can from her."

"So, did you learn anything new tonight?"

Eric took out the tin of coffee. "No, but I need to keep probing. She's bound to slip up sooner or later. But I do have something else to discuss."

Her interest piqued, Meg uncrossed her arms and sat straight. "You do? What?"

"Soon as we get our drinks."

While the coffee perked, he tucked a cushion behind her back and put her injured leg on the footstool. "You need to take care of yourself."

Meg hid a smile. "Why are you being so solicitous?"

"There you go again, impressing me with your vocabulary. I want to help, because this is the second time you've been in trouble here, and I feel responsible."

At his grim reminder, she sobered and looked away. "Not your fault. I'm here because I need to be."

"I know." His voice dropped a notch. "Me, too."

A few minutes later, he carried two steaming mugs into the living room. He handed her one and then sat beside her. "Now we can talk. Still, we'd better cozy up." Lifting an eyebrow, he pointed to the seascape and scooted closer.

His nearness raised an alarm, but other than climbing onto the arm of the sofa, she had no place to go. "So, what do you want to talk about?"

He sipped his coffee. "What we found today. The plank might be a door. We need to return and check it out."

Meg nodded. "What do you think might be inside? A hiding place for drugs?"

"Drugs are a good possibility, but we need proof." He shot her a glance. "I have more to talk about, if you want to hear."

"Of course, I do." His sharing meant he trusted her, and they truly were working together.

He set his mug on the coffee table and pulled several folded pieces of paper from his shirt pocket. "The first night we saw the two people in the woods? Next day, I searched the area and found these."

"So that's why you took so long returning the lunch things to Laureen."

"Right." He unfolded the papers and handed her the one on top.

She studied the paper. "Looks like a map. Crudely drawn, but includes some street names." She squinted at the wobbly printing. "'Las Vegas Boulevard.'"

"Yes, and check out this one. I think it has a street named 'Broad.'" He traced his forefinger along a line on the second piece of paper.

Meg leaned closer and peered at the spot he indicated. "Uh huh, and the intersecting line has a number. I think it's four."

"Fourth Street?"

Understanding dawned, and Meg pressed a finger to her cheek. "If this is a map...downtown Seattle has a Broad Street, which intersects with Fourth Avenue East. Hmmm, Seattle Center is there. And the Space Needle. Why would someone have a crudely-drawn map of Seattle Center?"

Eric stroked his chin. "Maybe the Center is a drug drop."

"What's on the other two papers?"

"More maps. But I don't recognize any of the streets." He handed her the last two sheets.

Meg studied each one from all angles. "I don't know where these locations are, either." She handed back the papers. "How can we find out?"

"I've been looking up the streets on the 'net. Takes a while."

"Which makes me wonder why anyone would draw crude maps such as these, instead of using cell phone apps."

Eric shrugged. "Who knows? Maybe the person wanted a back-up in case he lost his phone. Maybe he was just amusing himself. Whatever, I've sent photos of the papers to my source."

She shifted to face him. "Ah, yes, your source. Why don't you ask him to research the people here, like you had him find out about me?"

He grinned. "I have."

"I should have known. You're sure keeping him busy."

"He's a good guy and a good friend. Discreet, too." He tucked the papers into his shirt pocket then fell silent.

She elbowed his side. "Won't you tell me what you found out?"

His eyes glittered in the lamplight. "Sure you want to hear?" He ran a finger down her arm.

Meg shivered and inched away. "Of course, I do."

"Okay...for starters, take Burke. He's twenty-seven and was born in a small town in Montana. Ran away from home as a teenager and traveled around the country with a religious cult. You know, the ones who drive those old VW vans painted with weird pictures and psychedelic colors?"

Meg nodded. "I see them in town, sometimes. The cults like to camp in the parks."

"Yeah. He left the group a few years ago when they came to Seattle. He lived on the streets, hanging out in the homeless shelters."

She took another sip of her coffee. "How'd he end up working for Carl?"

"I'm not sure. But he's the kind of employee you'd want if you were doing something illegal." Eric slid his arm along the back of the sofa behind Meg and massaged her shoulder.

She briefly closed her eyes. His touch felt good. Too good. She swallowed. "And Jones? Did you find out about him?"

"Some. He's Nootlinga. He and Norrie must have

known each other at the tribe's casino. Norrie was a blackjack dealer, and Jones worked as a bouncer."

"I wonder how Carl and Jones connected." Still preoccupied by Eric's idle caresses, Meg struggled to keep her mind on their conversation.

"Probably through the charitable work Carl does at the res." Eric brushed a lock of her hair behind her ear. "Nice ears. Delicate."

His breath warmed her cheek, yet she shivered. "They are not."

"What? Not nice? Or not delicate? How would you know, anyway? You can't see 'em from my vantage point." He trailed his finger along her neck. "Nice neck, too."

Meg wanted to shift away, but she had no place to go, especially since he'd captured her shoulders. "Ah, who else did you find out about?"

"Okay, okay." Eric leaned back and blew out a deep breath. "How 'bout Lester? He's the typical computer nerd. Graduated high school and college with good grades. Worked for several of Seattle's high-tech outfits before hiring on with Carl a few years ago. Nothing suspicious about him, except he's made several trips to Canada in the past few months."

Meg's mind whirled with all the new information. "Arranging for drug smuggling? He's supposed to have a girlfriend there. Maybe she's involved."

"Don't know. Could be, or could be perfectly innocent."

"Were the trips part of his job for Carl?"

"That I don't know, either."

She heard the frustration in his voice. "How about Helen?" She cast him a sideways glance.

He picked up her hand and rubbed his thumb along the back. "You'd love to know about her, wouldn't you?"

"I know *you* would." She snatched away her hand.

"Helen was the All-American girl. High school cheerleader, college sorority girl, fraternity sweetheart. Married a football pro who turned out to be a wife abuser. After several restraining orders, she finally divorced him."

Meg raised her eyebrows. "She never mentioned being married. Not to me, anyway."

"Not to me, either. Probably not something she wants to talk about. She started with Fortune Industries as a secretary in Public Relations and worked her way up to running the PR department."

"Impressive. And she seems loyal to Carl."

"Carl has a way of inspiring loyalty among his employees. Maybe he pays them well. Maybe they just like him."

"Addie said Helen was involved with someone who died. She never mentioned her loss to me, even though we discussed relationships a time or two."

Eric frowned. "She didn't confide in me, either."

"Hmmm, a secret affair. Who else did you find out about?"

Eric looked at the ceiling. "Let's see…ah, Norm and Addie. Married for thirty-five years. Two sons and a daughter, grown and living elsewhere. Norm is Carl's chief liaison for his overseas operations."

"Which are?"

"Mainly building factories in other countries for our outsourcing, a highly controversial subject, as you probably know. But outsourcing makes money. And

Carl does love money."

"Mmmm, it sure bought him a fancy yacht. And this island." Had Johnny ever visited Gemini? Was that how he learned the island had a secret?

"You got that right. But back to Norm and Addie. They've been all over the world. My source couldn't find anything about either of them to indicate any shady dealings, but with their mobility, they certainly have enough opportunity." Eric reached for her hand again.

She drew away, but not fast enough.

He gripped her fingers. "Uh uh, if you wanta hear everything, you need to indulge me."

"You're impossible." But, finding the connection comforting, she let her hand stay in his.

"Hang on, I'm almost done. Kent Gheller's the only one left."

"Another loyal employee, or so he seems."

"Kent is from Germany. He came to this country as a young man and earned a business degree at a Midwestern university. He worked for various companies until hooking up with Carl."

She sighed and blew out a breath. "He always looks so sad. His eyes, especially. Maybe his sadness has to do with what happened to his wife's family. Helen said they were killed in Sukarla."

"Hey, Helen's been a better source for you than for me." He gave a low chuckle.

"Because with you, she has her mind on something else."

"Yeah, well, I can't help it if I'm irresistible."

Shaking her head, she sniffed. "'Insufferable' might be a better term, but we were talking about Kent…"

"Right. I haven't decided what I think about him. But, geez, we have enough to keep us busy, and you're tired, aren't you?"

"I am." She may have been tired, but his nearness and his continual caresses kept her nerves thrumming.

"Poor Meg, you've been through another rough time today. You'll feel better when your ankle heals." His voice lowered. "I can't make it heal any faster than nature intends, but I know another kind of healing."

Her breath caught. "What's that?"

"This." He grasped her chin and turned her face to his.

She could have pulled away, but she didn't. Instead, she leaned into him. His mouth closed over hers, his lips warm and soft. He groaned and wrapped her in his arms, caressing her back from her shoulders to her waist.

Desire poured through her. Her cheeks flamed, and she was sure he must be able to feel her heat. She ran her hands along his shoulders and his arms, over corded muscles and solid flesh. She reveled in the touch, taste, and feel of him. Then, attempting to snuggle even closer, she twisted—and pain stabbed her ankle. "Ouch."

He drew back. "Did I hurt you?"

"No, it's my ankle." She leaned forward and rubbed the injury, the ice pack fallen to the side.

Keeping one arm around her shoulders, he put his other hand over hers and deepened the massage. "I shouldn't take advantage of you. I'm sorry."

"My fault as much as yours." Feeling the pain ease, she relaxed against him again.

He sat back, too, and drew her close. "But you've

already told me you don't want to get involved."

"It's not you. I mean, don't take my reluctance personally."

He laughed. "How should I take it?"

"I'm not someone who takes sex lightly. Oh, I sound prissy, don't I?" She pressed her fingers to her lips and shot him a sideways glance.

"Yeah, but I'm listening."

The sincerity in his voice encouraged her to continue. "My emotions need to be involved. I want to have sex with someone I love, someone I want to marry."

"Okay, if that works for you. But I also think sex can be a healing. One of my favorite songs is 'Sexual Healing.' I have Marvin Gaye's version on a CD." He hummed a few bars.

"Yes, I know the song. So that's all sex is to you? A healing of sorts?"

"That's pretty much it."

She heaved a deep sigh. "We are miles apart, aren't we?"

"We are. But at least we're both being honest. Honesty is worth something, isn't it?"

Chapter Fourteen

Eric rolled over in bed, picked up his wristwatch from the nightstand, and checked the luminous dial. Three-thirty. After tossing and turning, he'd finally managed to settle down and drop off to sleep. Why had he awakened now?

He listened. Silence. Even though Carl and his guests partied hearty, by now they all should be tucked away for the night. He turned over again and punched up his pillow. What bothered him? The talk he and Meg had tonight?

Trusting women and their affections always proved difficult. The shrink he visited a couple years ago told him his fear was because his mother had abandoned him and his father when he was only five. Okay, maybe so. And, no, he couldn't change. Didn't really want to change. He liked his life the way it was.

He'd seen the raw desire in Meg's eyes, though. She could preach all she wanted to about her reasons for making love, but she wanted him. And he wanted her.

He could blame his desire on being isolated on the island. And on not having seen Sally lately. Yeah, he'd call her tomorrow. He needed to touch bases and set the anchor where it belonged.

****

Meg opened her eyes to sunlight streaming through

the crack in the blinds, and for a moment, she thought she was in her Seattle apartment. Then, as she turned over, she glimpsed her suitcase in the corner and remembered she was on Gemini Island. Gemini, where she'd come to find out the truth about Johnny and Alyssa's accident. Where she'd met Eric Richards. And last night…oh, last night she'd wanted so badly to make love with him. If she'd given in, she might have him beside her now, filling the other side of the bed with his long, lean body.

No use thinking about what might have been. She'd stand by her decision. With a sigh, she pushed back the covers and swung her legs over the side. Easing to her feet, she gingerly put partial weight on the sore ankle. No pain. She put her full weight on her foot and took a step. Okay, sore, but not bad. She'd walk just fine today.

In the bathroom, she studied her reflection in the mirror. Hair a mess, face flushed from sleep; otherwise, she looked no different than before…before Eric. Even though they hadn't made love, something inside her had changed. A door to desires long dormant had opened. Trouble was, she couldn't cross the threshold. Correction—she wouldn't allow herself to cross it.

Thirty minutes later, Meg entered the main house's dining room.

Kent sat alone at the table, bony arms sticking out of his short-sleeved shirt. He looked at her with eyes that matched the color of his Bloody Mary drink.

"Bad night?" she asked.

He rubbed long fingers over his forehead. "I should know better than to try to keep up with Carl when he's in party mode."

Meg gazed around the room. "So where is Carl?"

"He's out jogging. I don't know how he does it." He took a swallow of his drink and made a sour face.

"Lester?"

"Sacked out on the patio. Don't know if he ever made it to bed or not. Helen's up, though. I passed Addie's and Norm's cottage, and she stuck her head out a window and said she'd be here in a while."

Meg sat across from him, picked up a silver carafe, and poured herself a cup of coffee. "You all do a good job keeping track of each other."

"We're a tight group. So what happened to you last night? You disappeared."

"I was tired. And my ankle hurt."

"Ah, yes, the ankle. How is it today? Didn't notice you limping when you came in."

She set the carafe back on the silver-plated tray and took a sip of coffee. "A little sore, but much better."

Kent frowned. "Couldn't have been too bad an injury."

"No, thankfully."

Addie arrived, wearing a floral print blouse over white slacks. Her red hair was neatly coifed, as usual, but her eyes looked puffy.

"Oh my, oh my, give me some coffee, quick." Addie grabbed a cup from the table and held it out for Kent to do the honors.

"What a day we had yesterday. Fun, fun, fun." She looked at Meg. "Didn't I tell you Carl's parties were the best?" She tilted her head. "But how would you know? You missed nearly everything. You weren't on the cruise, and I didn't see you last night after dinner."

"I really needed to rest, and Burke drove me to my

cottage."

"I see." Addie raised her eyebrows.

The woman didn't sound convinced, but Meg wasn't about to volunteer any more to satisfy her curiosity.

"Where's Norm?" Kent pulled the celery stalk from his Bloody Mary, took a bite, and grimaced. "Ugh, who invented this stupid drink?"

Addie plopped into a chair. "Norm's stomach is bothering him this morning. I'll take him something to eat when I go back."

Lester joined them, his hair its usual bird's nest, his denim shirt and jeans looking as though they'd been slept in. Carl would be lucky to get any work out of either him or Kent today.

"Don't anybody talk to me until I have some juice." Lester slumped to the sideboard and with a shaky hand poured a glass of orange juice from a ceramic pitcher. He tipped back his head, took a long drink, and then wobbled over and sat next to Meg.

Addie's gaze roved from one to the other. "Carl certainly has an interesting group of people this time around."

No one responded.

Finally, Lester heaved a sigh. "Okay, I'll bite. Whatcha got, Addie?"

Narrowing her gaze, Addie leaned over the table. "I saw something very interesting last night." Then she sat back and sipped her coffee.

Lester rolled his eyes. "Just tell us and get it over with, okay?"

Addie huffed. "Please allow me my moment, Mr. Lester. As you know, or maybe you don't, our cottage is next to Eric's."

Meg's stomach tensed. Was Addie about to say she saw Eric enter her cottage? Or come out? What?

"And guess who I saw going in around midnight?" Addie looked from one to the other.

"Burke," Lester guessed. "Or Jones." He snapped his fingers. "Dang, I knew it. And just when I hoped they'd pay that kind of attention to me."

"Don't be ridiculous." Addie wrinkled her nose. "No, I saw Helen." Eyes gleaming, she sat back, clamped her jaw shut, and folded her arms.

Meg stiffened and choked on a swallow of coffee.

"You okay?" Lester patted her on the back.

"Yes, yes, I'm fine." She pressed her napkin to her mouth.

Kent's eyebrows shot up. "Really, Addie? Or did you just need some drama and so you imagined you saw Helen?"

"I did not imagine her." Addie turned to Meg. "Maybe you saw her, too. Your cottage is on the other side of his."

"Around midnight?" Keeping her expression neutral, Meg met Addie's gaze. "No, I was fast asleep by then."

"So why were you out nosing around?" Kent asked Addie.

Addie tilted her chin. "I wasn't nosing around." She grinned. "Although I will admit to being nosy on occasion. No, last night, on the way to our cottage, Norm and I saw Helen on the path ahead of us. But apparently she didn't see us. And I don't think Eric saw us, either. He let her inside really fast and slammed the door."

Helen arrived, and conversation abruptly ceased. She stopped and looked around with narrowed eyes. "You were talking about me."

Addie shook her head. "No, no, my dear. We're just a bit the worse for wear is all. Sit down and be miserable with us." She nodded to an empty place at the table.

"I'll sit, but I'm far from miserable."

Helen looked as cool as ever in a blue cotton top and matching slacks. A white belt emphasized her small waist and round hips. Her blonde hair fell smoothly from its central part, curving under her chin like twin commas. Meg remembered what Eric had said last night about Helen—cheerleader, sorority girl, and fraternity sweetheart. Yes, she easily could have been all of those.

Helen swept to the sideboard and filled a plate with food from the silver warming dishes, an act none of the others had yet done.

While the woman's back was turned, Addie winked at her tablemates.

Helen brought her plate to the table and sat. "I'm starved." She picked up her fork.

A collective groan issued around the table.

Eric strode in. "Good morning, everyone."

Except for Helen's cheerful, "Hello, Eric," the replies were incoherent mumbles.

Eric went to the sideboard and filled his plate with eggs, hash browns, and toast. He sat beside Meg and looked around at the others. "So, how's everybody this morning?"

"Wiped," Lester said.

"I'm fine." Helen beamed at Eric.

Kent ducked his head and mumbled into his drink.

Like a table tennis ball, Addie's gaze darted from Eric to Helen.

Eric turned to Meg. "How's your ankle?"

"Better, thank you," she said in a crisp tone.

Eric spread his napkin on his lap.

Meg felt a subtle pressure on her knee. A moment passed before she realized Eric's hand caused the sensation. She huffed under her breath. The nerve of him, playing with her under the table when last night... When last night, what? She knew nothing about last night, except what had happened between the two of them. She jerked her leg from his grasp. He didn't miss a beat, didn't even glance her way. Her rejection didn't faze him. Why should it, when he apparently had Helen to help him practice his sexual healing? Meg put down her cup. "If you will excuse me, I need to report to work."

"Without eating?" Helen inquired.

"I'm really not hungry. Carl's put us on a deadline, you know, and I don't want to get behind." She stood and pushed in her chair.

Helen turned to Eric. "Will you be leaving soon to work, too? I was hoping you'd join me for a walk on the beach."

Meg was out the door before Eric replied.

****

In the museum workroom, Meg studied an index card detailing a Kwakiutl cloak made of shredded cedar bark. She entered the data into her computer, placed the index card in the metal file, and sat back. The peace and quiet were wonderful, just what she needed. She liked being alone, even though the huge building was always a bit spooky. Alone was what she wanted. Work would help her to heal, not mindless groping with a man who was still virtually a stranger and who apparently kept his options open where women were concerned.

However, she couldn't help wondering when Eric would appear. She checked her wristwatch. An hour had passed since she'd arrived. Maybe he wouldn't show up at all. Maybe he'd taken a walk with Helen instead.

So? All the better for her solitude. She picked up another card, scanned the information, and began to type.

"Hey, Meg, I'm here."

Eric. She bent over the keyboard and punched the keys. Risking a sideways glance, she saw he carried a canvas tote.

"Figured you might need something to keep you going." He pulled a thermos from the bag and held it up.

She met his gaze. "That was thoughtful." Mixed emotions, from gratitude to annoyance, flooded her. And, as always, an awareness of his physical appeal. His hair brushed smoothly back from his high forehead. His T-shirt tightly stretched across his chest. His jeans were snug over a flat stomach and firm thighs. Did he buy his clothing a size too small, just to show off his body? She wouldn't put it past him.

He set the tote and thermos on a corner of her desk, took out two mugs, and filled them with coffee. He handed her one of the mugs. "Here you go."

Careful to keep from touching his fingers, she accepted the cup. The rich aroma filled the air. She took a sip and sighed. Coffee hit the spot.

He pulled a foil-wrapped package from the tote and unwrapped it to reveal several slices of toast. "Thought you might be hungry."

"I am." She took a piece of toast and bit into it. Crisp and smothered with butter, the toast, too, was just what she needed.

Several moments passed while they both drank their coffee, and Meg ate two pieces of toast. Then he leaned down and said in her ear, "We need to talk. Now. Outside."

She breathed in the scent of his aftershave. "What about?"

"Business."

"All right." She set down her mug, saved her document on the computer, and followed him out the sliding glass doors. A light breeze cooled her cheeks and raised goose bumps along her arms. She crossed to the edge of the patio and gazed into the forest.

He approached from behind, placed his hands on her shoulders, and gently turned her around. "You're pissed at me. Why? I thought we parted on good terms last night."

"As good terms as you had later with Helen?" Meg gritted her teeth. Why couldn't she control her emotions where he was concerned?

He let his arms drop to his sides. His eyelids closed for a second and then opened again. "How'd you know about that?"

Stepping away, she hugged her waist. "Addie told everyone at breakfast, before you came in."

"Addie, again." Eric wrinkled his nose. "The woman drives me nuts. How did she know?"

"She and Norm were behind Helen on the path

when Helen turned in at your cottage. They saw you open the door and let her inside."

He turned away and stared into the forest.

Her heart constricted. "So, Addie was right. You did see Helen last night."

Eric nodded. "For a little while. But nothing happened. Not what you're upset about, anyway."

"You know something?" Meg stuck her chin in the air. "I don't care. You're free to do as you like. So am I."

"You're right." His eyes darkened. "But *nothing happened* between me and Helen." He ground out the words.

"Then why did she come to your cottage at midnight?"

He spread his hands. "She missed me…"

Meg rolled her eyes. "Oh, how sweet. She missed you."

"…at the party, and worried I might be sick."

"You let her in."

"Of course, I did." He frowned. "I'm not rude. Besides, allowing her in was an opportunity to get some useful information."

"And did you get any?" Realizing how that sounded, she quickly added, "Information, I mean."

He chuckled. "You never know what might be important. Anyway, we had a drink, talked a while, and she left. Satisfied?"

"Yes. No. Oh, I don't know. I wish I'd never become involved with you. Why did I?" The question was more for her than for him.

"You couldn't help yourself. We were fated to meet."

She glimpsed his teasing grin. "Yeah, right. But, anyway, what you and Helen did—or did not do—is none of my business. I'm sorry. I just have this…problem." She ran a hand over her forehead.

"Were you jealous when you were married?" His tone was softer now.

"Not at first. After a year or so, I was. I don't know if he was seeing other women or not. I never had any proof. I think my *problem* might have to do with my father always preferring my sister Angie to me. At least, I thought he did."

"Younger or older sister?"

"Younger. Dad's gone now. And although Angie and I aren't close, we're friends. But with Johnny, the drinking is what really killed our relationship—for me, anyway. But this, this *thing,* whatever it is, with you is different. We aren't married, we aren't engaged, we aren't *anything* to each other." She threw up her hands. "And why am I telling you all this, anyway?"

He stepped close and laid a hand on her shoulder. "Relax. I'm glad you're telling me. I have a few scars from my childhood, too. And, everything that's happened to you recently has made you vulnerable."

"Yes, I suppose so. Let's move on, okay?"

He raised one eyebrow. "You're still with me on our quest?"

"Of course, I am."

"Good. We'll shelve all the personal stuff for now. Why don't you take a load off?" He nodded at the wrought iron table and chairs.

Meg sat and rested her folded arms on the table. A light breeze cooled her cheeks, and birds twittered from the nearby pine trees. "Okay, what's next on our agenda?"

Eric slipped into the chair across from her. He glanced around then leaned close and lowered his voice. "We need to go back to the mountain and find out what's behind the door."

"Did you mention the mountain to Helen?"

"I told her I wondered why Carl keeps that part of the island off-limits. I asked if she knew any reason, other than the one he gives, that the area is undeveloped and therefore a possible liability."

"And did she?"

"No. But she said he disappears in that direction frequently, usually in the early evening. So, we'll take a little trip there this afternoon."

"What if someone sees us? The island has eyes everywhere."

"I've thought of the perfect cover. Here's what we'll do…"

****

Later that afternoon, Meg paced her living room as she waited for Eric. Why had she let him talk her into going along with his wild scheme? When she first heard his plan, she thought it would work. Now, she feared the scheme would backfire and blow their covers. Still, if their trip led her closer to discovering the truth about her beloved daughter's death, it would be worth the risk.

Eric arrived. "Ready to go? Got your camera?"

"In my backpack." She patted the strap on her shoulder.

"Wear your camera around your neck, like I'm wearing these binoculars." He fingered the pair against his chest. "Makes us look more authentic. Besides, you really will take pictures. Here, I'll get the camera."

She turned to allow access to her backpack. "Is our cover all set?"

"Yeah. I told Laureen we wanted to do some bird watching. And no, we wouldn't go near the mountain. She told me about an eagle's aerie on the north side and gave me a birdwatcher's guide from Carl's library." He pulled out the camera and hung it around her neck.

His hands lingered on her shoulders, sending a rush of heat down her spine. She struggled to keep her mind on their purpose. "What are the others doing now?"

"Working in Carl's office."

"Jones and Burke?"

He zipped up her backpack. "Jones is on an errand to Orcas. I don't know where Burke is. We'll hope we don't run into him. We have to hurry, though."

They set off, trudging along a path leading to the northern part of the island. When they were well out of sight of the house, they veered to the west. The dense woods allowed little light to filter through the trees. The gloom matched her mood. Bird watching? This was crazy.

Eric stopped and pointed to a bird sitting on the branch of a fir tree. "There's a bird. Take a picture, so we have something to show for our trip."

Meg dutifully aimed her camera at the tiny gray bird just before it flapped its wings and took off.

They followed one path and then another. None of the routes appeared well traveled. "I don't see how you can find your way," she complained to his back as she followed him along a narrow track.

"Easy. Just keep heading for the ol' mountain."

"I mean, how will we ever find the exact place

where we were before?"

"That won't be a problem. Trust me, I have a good instinct for remembering locations. And this helps." He held up a small compass.

Sure enough, five minutes and several bird pictures later, they stood in the clearing they'd found on their previous trip. Eric nodded to the base of the mountain. "Okay, let's find the plank."

They went to work, pulling away branches and digging through the underbrush.

"Ah ha," Eric said after a few minutes, "here it is." He stepped aside and pointed to the plank embedded in the side of the mountain. "I'm betting this is a door." Eric was right—removing the plywood revealed a crude hole into the mountain. He pulled out his flashlight and shone the light inside. "Looks like a cave."

She peered over his shoulder. "Can you see anything?"

"Not from here. We'll have to go in." He glanced at her. "You game?"

"Of course." Meg's heart pounded as she followed Eric through the narrow doorway into the mountain's interior. A wave of damp, musty air, carrying the scent of rotten wood, engulfed her.

Eric swept his light over the area. "Someone's done a bit of work. The walls are shored up with wooden beams."

"Maybe it's a bomb shelter."

"Probably not. If that were the case, the walls would be concrete-lined and stocked with provisions and creature comforts. I don't see anything like that. But we'll look a little farther."

Meg stepped to one side, and the toe of her shoe hit

something hard. She looked down to see a shadowy form. "Here's something."

Eric played his light over the object. "An old log. No, more than that."

Stooping, Meg looked closer and recognized a carving on the log that resembled a fox's head.

"A totem," they both said at once.

"A really old, beat up one," Eric added.

"That must account for the smell of rotting wood." Meg fanned the air with her hand.

Eric focused the light on the top of the pole. "Looks like an eagle carving."

"Uh huh. Wings spread, ready to take off."

Eric examined the ground around the pole. "I see a hammer. And a chisel and a knife. I'd say someone's restoring the totem."

"But why in secret?"

"Good question. Is Carl doing the work? If so, why not at the museum, where he'd have plenty of space and a whole lot better light."

Meg knelt and ran her fingers over the rough wood of the eagle's wing. "Indians didn't hide treasure in totems, did they?"

"Not that I know of. Even so, once you removed the treasure, why go to the trouble of restoring the pole?"

"Unless you're someone like Carl, who collects Indian artifacts." Meg stood and brushed the wood dust from her hands.

"True. But, still, why all the secrecy and security?"

They examined the rest of the room but found only a few more tools and cans of paint.

Eric took a step toward the opening. "We'd better

get out of here, in case Carl decides to make an early visit."

Outside the cave, they pulled the plywood panel into place and covered it with the foliage. As she placed one of the branches, she heard the nearby bushes rustle. "Someone's coming."

Eric scooped up the rest of the greenery and tossed it onto the door. "Okay, back to the path. Hurry."

Meg grabbed her camera and had barely stepped onto the path when a voice called, "Hello, there!"

Chapter Fifteen

Meg held her breath, waiting to see who would appear. The person turned out to be Addie. Dressed in khaki shorts and blouse, a wide-brimmed hat tied under her chin, and carrying a tote, she looked like someone on an African safari.

"Hey, Addie." Eric waved. "I thought you were stuck in the meeting with Carl and the others."

"I joined them for a while, but I got bored and decided to go for a hike. You look busy." She gestured at Eric's binoculars and Meg's camera.

Eric nodded. "Bird watching."

"Ah." Addie raised an eyebrow. "Find any?"

"Several. Meg took pictures. I'll download and print them when we get back, if you're interested."

Addie sniffed and fiddled with the tie under her chin. "Not particularly. Birds aren't my thing."

"Where are you headed?" Meg asked.

"To the beach on the north side." Addie looked around and wrinkled her nose. "I wish Carl would make a map of all the pathways on the island. Then maybe people wouldn't get lost."

"Lost? Did someone get lost?" Eric leaned toward Addie.

Addie pressed her fingers to her lips. "I don't know. I'm just assuming."

"We're on our way back, if you want to join us."

Eric nodded to the path.

Addie shook her head. "I'm determined to find the beach. See y'all at dinner." She gave a little wave and stalked off.

Meg waited until Addie was out of earshot and then turned to Eric. "Do you think she bought our story?"

"Who knows?" Eric shrugged. "Addie might know more than she lets on."

"She doesn't miss much." She glanced in the direction Addie took.

"She's a busybody."

Meg adjusted her backpack. "Maybe Carl asked her to follow us, to give Jones and Burke a break."

"Yeah, they're kinda obvious. But if she followed us, she must've seen us enter the hole in the mountain." He gestured to the now-hidden plank.

"I wonder what Carl will do when—if—he finds out. Do you think he'd go so far as to fire us?"

"I hope not, but that remains to be seen. Come on, we'll go back. We're done here."

"What should we do next?" Meg asked later when they returned to their cottages.

Eric accompanied her up the walk to her front door. "There's a whole other side of the mountain we haven't explored yet."

"Yes, we might find more clues there. When can we go?"

"I'm not sure. We'll lie low for a couple of days. Carl should make a trip to the mainland sometime this week. Best to do our sleuthing when he's gone."

****

The week passed, with Carl and the others

remaining on the island. Along with Eric, Meg concentrated on her work at the museum.

On Friday evening after dinner, instead of joining the others for their usual post-dinner patio party, Meg excused herself and headed for Wolf House. She looked forward to some alone time.

Eric soon caught up. "You look tired tonight," he said, matching her steps on the winding path.

Meg shrugged. "Not so much tired, as discouraged. We haven't found anything conclusive. I'm wondering if we ever will, or if this trip has been a waste of time."

"I'm discouraged, too. But we still haven't checked out the water side of the mountain." He gestured over his shoulder to Mt. Gemini looming in the background.

"We may not get a chance to."

"Hey, let's think positive, okay?"

They reached her cottage, where the wolf totem, as usual, stood guard. Meg pulled her key from her jacket pocket and turned to say goodnight.

"Wait." He laid a hand on her arm. "How 'bout I come in for a while? I hate to leave you feeling so down."

Meg tightened her grip on her key. "Coming in is a bad idea."

"Why?"

"You know very well why." She tossed him a stern look.

He grinned and brushed a lock of hair from her forehead. "Talk, that's all. And maybe a drink."

The warmth of his fingers spread throughout her body. She swallowed hard. "Um, all I have is coffee."

"Coffee's good. Come on, don't be inhospitable."

"My, my, talk about a big vocabulary—"

His eyes glinted with teasing. "Glad you're impressed. Gotta be on my toes to compete with you." He held out his hand. "Key, please."

She placed her hand over his and let the key slip from her fingers.

He unlocked the door and, following close on her heels, gave her a gentle nudge inside. Meg hung her jacket in the closet, and Eric went to the kitchen.

On his way past the counter, he flipped on the radio. Sounds of classical music filled the air. He switched the dial, stopping at one playing soft rock.

Meg sank onto the sofa, leaned back, and closed her eyes. Fatigue washed over her. Given her mixed feelings toward Eric, allowing him to come in was a bad decision. Why hadn't she insisted he go to his own cottage and leave her alone? A few minutes later, the smell of freshly brewed coffee reached her nose. She opened her eyes to find Eric holding out a steaming mug.

"Here you go."

She couldn't help smiling as she accepted the cup. "You make me feel like a little kid, sometimes, with your caretaking."

"I had a good role model in my dad. He was there for me, all the way, until I grew up." He slanted her a glance. "Want to hear more?"

"Yes, go on." Talking might be a way to avoid physical involvement.

Eric sat beside her and propped his ankle on his knee. "He took me to baseball games, and when I wanted to learn how to play, he taught me. He showed me how to hit and pitch a ball, and how to run the bases. He let me join a youth football league and never missed any of my games." He sipped his coffee. "I'll never forget the times we had together. Sure, some teaching was involved, but more important was his just being with me."

"He sounds like a great father." Eric never talked much about his personal life and hearing his nostalgic story made her feel close.

"He was."

"What about your mother?"

Eric shook his head and gave a mirthless laugh. "She took off when I was five years old. I barely remember her."

His unexpected and flatly stated admission gave her a start. She pressed a hand against her chest. "I'm sorry. Her leaving must have been tough for you and your dad."

He made a dismissive wave. "Thanks for the sympathy, but we were talking about positive experiences. Now, you take a turn. Tell me about an important adult in your life."

He had shared with her, so why not? She took a moment to gather her thoughts. "I had a great relationship with my Aunt Belle, my mother's younger sister. She was beautiful, with long dark hair and elegant clothes. And so kind and thoughtful." She closed her eyes for a moment and pictured her beloved relative.

"Sounds like a dream auntie."

"She was. She gave me her old clothes for playing dress-up." Meg let her gaze go blurry so she could remember. "We'd fix each other's hair, and she'd let me use her makeup. I always felt very glamorous—and very loved—after being with Aunt Belle."

Eric put his arm around Meg's shoulders. "Are you two still in contact?"

A lump rose in Meg's throat, and she waited several seconds before continuing. "She died when I was eleven."

"What happened? Or is it too painful to talk about?"

"No, I'll tell you." She leaned against him, taking comfort in the firmness of his body. "Her death was tragic. She had moved from Seattle to San Francisco, where her fiancé lived. She was riding the trolley, on the way to her job at a department store. A bus hit the trolley. The car jumped the track, and a lot of riders, including Aunt Belle, were thrown off. She fell into the path of a delivery truck. They rushed her to the hospital, but she lived only a few hours." Tears welled in her eyes. She brushed them away with the back of her hand.

He whipped out his handkerchief and dabbed at the tears. "Hey, I didn't mean to make you sad."

"I know you didn't." She nodded as she sagged back against the couch. "I'm sad because Aunt Belle is lost to me, like Johnny and Alyssa. And when I think about never seeing them again—especially Alyssa, but Johnny, too—my heart breaks."

He tucked away his handkerchief. "I feel the same way. I'd like nothing more right now than to see Norrie walk through the door. Yeah, I'd love that to happen. But it ain't gonna, and I have to live with that fact."

"That doesn't mean we can't be sorry."

"Of course not. If you want to be sad tonight, do it, and I'm here for you, okay?" He drew her against him.

"Okay," she whispered, resting her head on his shoulder.

Neither spoke, with the only sound the soft music in the background. A sense of peace stole over Meg. She and Eric may disagree about many things, but the shared sorrow over the loss of their loved ones brought them together.

Presently, Eric planted a gentle kiss on Meg's forehead and withdrew his arm from around her shoulders. "See ya tomorrow. But if something comes up later, and you need me, give a holler."

"I will. And, Eric?"

"Yeah?" He stood and gazed at her, a gleam lighting his eyes.

Leaning forward, she had to smile. "No, not what you think. I only wanted to thank you—for your understanding."

"You're welcome." He gave a solemn nod and left.

Unable to resist, she went to the window and with a catch in her throat, watched every step until he was out of sight. Earlier, she hadn't wanted him to come in. Now, she didn't want him to leave.

****

A few days later, this time after spending the evening sitting on the patio with the others, Meg and Eric again walked along the path to their cottages. Meg gazed at the bright moonlight peeking through the trees and then at the shadows dancing across the ground. She wished she could relax and enjoy the warm night, but her nerves were on edge.

Several times during the evening, Meg caught Helen's gaze on her. At first, she ignored the look, which she could not interpret, anyway. But, after a while, Meg's patience was stretched to the limit, and she met the other woman's look head-on.

Helen scowled. Then her scowl faded, and she smiled.

Meg nodded and smiled back. Still, she found Helen's strange behavior unsettling.

"We need to go back to the mountain."

Eric's declaration broke into her thoughts. She glanced over her shoulder to where the peak stood silhouetted against the night sky. "So you keep telling me, but the opportunity never arises. Carl's been staying on the island, along with everyone else, and Jones and Burke continue to lurk and pop out when you least expect them."

He gripped her elbow to guide them around a bend. "I could throw caution to the wind, as they say, and go by myself. You don't have to go."

Meg stiffened. "You always want to leave me out. Of course, I want to go. I'm in this just as much as you are."

"Relax." He patted her shoulder. "I know you are, but you've had a couple accidents already, and I don't want anything else to happen."

Her tension eased, and she flashed him a smile. "Thanks. I appreciate your concern." She cared what happened to him, too. She wasn't in love, but her feelings were far different from when they first met. Then, she was put off by what she perceived as arrogance and an overbearing ego.

Now she saw a different side of him. Okay, so maybe sharing kisses had something to do with her new feelings. But over the past few weeks, they'd come to know each other. A common goal had brought them together, and a bond was formed. Plus, sharing experiences from their pasts helped to understand each other better.

She struggled to get a grip on her emotions. Her focus needed to be their problem, not what might or might not be happening between them. "Are you looking for anything specific on the other side of the mountain?"

"I thought we might find another cave where drugs are delivered...if drugs are involved. I wish we knew." Frowning, he made a fist and pounded his palm.

He could be right about the need to explore the mountain's other side, but the thought of entering another dark, dank cave gave her the creeps.

They turned a corner, bringing the cottages and the totem pole guards into view. Tonight, the wolf's bared teeth and staring eyes appeared more menacing than ever. Meg shivered and hugged her arms.

"You cold?" Eric rubbed her shoulder.

His fingers were warm through the thin fabric of her blouse. "No, Mr. Wolf gave me a start." She pointed to the totem. "Sometimes he's benign and welcoming, and other times, like now, he's evil and frightening."

Eric tilted his head to study the totem. "I think the carver made him capable of both to remind us the world has both good and evil."

"I didn't know you had a philosophical side," she teased as they continued on to her cottage.

He gave a short laugh. "There's a lot you don't know about me. But don't be scared tonight. I'm right next door. Or...I could be closer. Hmmm?" He trailed his finger from her shoulder down her bare arm.

Her throat tight, she pulled away and stepped onto her cottage's doorstep.

Grasping her shoulders, he turned her to face him. "Think about it."

"About what?" She'd better make sure they were talking about the same thing.

"You know. How it would be with us."

His gaze held hers. Heat flowed back and forth between them. "I hate to admit you're tempting me."

"Good." He grinned. "Stop worrying and enjoy." Sliding his arm around her waist, he pulled her close and nuzzled her neck.

She closed her eyes and gave in to the heady sensation of being in his arms again. Maybe tonight she would let him come inside…She opened her eyes and, gazing over his shoulder, glimpsed a light shining through the trees. "Eric! Look!"

"Don't bother me, I'm busy."

Pressing against his chest, she struggled to pull away. "I see a light on the mountain. A blinking light, just like we saw that night from the beach."

Eric slowly raised his head and faced the mountain. "You're right. I see it, too."

"This could be important." She gripped his shoulder.

"Yeah. Rotten timing, but duty calls. We gotta check it out." He pointed toward the door. "Put on some sturdy shoes and a jacket. Grab a flashlight. If you didn't bring one, then I'll have an extra. Come to my place when you're ready."

"Are we going through the woods again?"

"No. By boat."

Chapter Sixteen

Ten minutes later, Meg and Eric hurried along the path leading to the boat docks. The wind whispered in the trees, and nocturnal animals skittered through the underbrush. Meg frequently glanced over her shoulder, expecting to see Burke or Jones behind them.

Eric took her hand. "Quit worrying. If we meet anyone, we'll say we're out for a walk, a perfectly logical excuse."

They reached the docks. Meg expected him to head for *Wave Catcher*, the boat they'd taken to Orcas Island. Instead, he stopped beside a rowboat. "No sense in alerting anyone with the noise of a motor."

Soon they were on the water. Eric sat in the middle plying the oars, and Meg occupied the stern. She huddled on the hard, wooden seat and gazed out to sea where vague shadows on the horizon represented other islands. Here and there, a light penetrated the darkness. This route was more dangerous than slogging through the woods. The woods offered hiding places, but here they were the proverbial sitting ducks. "What will we do when we get there?" she asked, breaking a lengthy silence.

He shrugged. "Don't know. We'll decide when the time comes."

She gave an exasperated sigh. "I hate not having a plan."

"I know." Eric steered them around a large piece of driftwood. "You want everything worked out ahead of time."

Meg idly watched the wood float by, bobbing and dipping in the water. "Yes, especially in a case like this."

"I prefer a wait-and-see attitude." On course again, Eric tugged the oars.

"Yes, well, we already know we have different styles. Vastly different."

"I wouldn't go so far as to say, 'vastly.' You talk as though we're miles apart."

She tore her gaze away from the water and faced him, arching an eyebrow. "Aren't we?"

"I don't think so."

"Why are we having this conversation, anyway?"

He grinned. "Something to talk about."

They both fell silent. After a while, she slanted him a glance. "I suppose you brought your gun."

"My gun?" Eric raised his eyebrows.

She gripped the rail and leaned forward. "I know you have one. That first night, in the woods, I felt something hard by your hip."

"You're sure what you felt was my gun?" His laughter rang out.

Meg felt her cheeks flush. "Oh, forget it."

He stopped laughing and nodded. "Okay, I do have a gun, just where you said. And around my neck I have night-vision binoculars, and in my jacket pocket, an infrared camera."

"So you're equipped to skulk at night." She leaned closer. "Who are you, really? I think you're a spy."

"I'm in the computer software business, like I told

you."

"Like I should believe you?"

He shrugged. "Suit yourself."

They reached the far side of the mountain. Eric dropped the oars and picked up his binoculars.

Meg studied the shoreline. Several yards of beach ended against a bank heavy with undergrowth. Beyond the bank rose the mountain. "I don't see anything out of the ordinary."

"I see a fishing boat." Eric lowered the binoculars and pointed out to sea.

Sure enough, a boat floated near the horizon. "You're right. But lots of boats pass by on their way to and from Canada."

"This one's a purse seiner, and it's not passing by; it's coming this way. Which means we'd better get out of sight."

Eric rowed to the shore. They dragged the boat onto the beach, shoved it behind a pile of large rocks, and then hid in the nearby underbrush.

Parting the branches, Eric again studied the water through his binoculars. "They've lowered a rowboat. It's heading for the island. Take a look." He passed her the glasses.

Meg peered through the lenses, adjusting the focus to fit her vision. The fishing boat was near enough to make out a dark hull with white trim. The rowboat was indeed on its way to Gemini. "Two people are in the rowboat."

"That's what I thought."

She lowered the glasses to find Eric capturing several pictures with his camera. A few minutes later, the rowboat reached Gemini's shore. Meg's pulse quickened. Were they about to discover something important?

The boat landed. Two figures jumped out and pulled the boat ashore.

Although Meg couldn't be positive, she guessed the two were both men. They wore knee-high boots, dark pants, and jackets. Caps with visors low on their foreheads hid their features.

"They're coming this way." Eric aimed his camera and took several shots.

"Oh, great." Meg scrunched farther down into the bushes. Her heart thudded.

The two came closer, their voices audible now.

Yes, they were male. She couldn't understand the language, but the sharp tones indicated an argument. She ventured a peek.

The shorter of the two motioned his companion toward the mountain, away from where Meg and Eric were hidden. The second man pointed to the sand.

"Oh, oh, I bet they spotted our footprints," Eric whispered.

Meg's heart hammered. What if they were discovered? How dangerous were these men?

"Stay down and keep quiet." Eric inched closer and put an arm around her waist.

Like a bloodhound with his nose to the scent, the taller man climbed the bank and approached their hideout.

The branches in front of Meg's face swayed. Sharp twigs dug into her cheek. Looking down, she saw the man's boot, close enough to reach out and touch the scuffed toe. Staring at the boot, she held her breath. Any moment now…

Just then, the man's companion called. The first man mumbled and then kicked the bushes, hitting Meg's knee.

She bit her lip to keep from crying out. Eric's arm around her tightened.

Finally, with a grunt, the man stomped off. He joined his partner, and their voices faded.

Meg sagged against Eric's shoulder.

"You did good," he whispered in her ear.

"Please don't tell me we're following them," she whispered back, too aware of her pounding heart.

"No, too dangerous."

The minutes ticked by. At last, one of the men tramped from the woods.

Peering through the foliage, Meg thought he was the one who nearly discovered them, but she couldn't be positive.

Eric picked up his camera and snapped a picture.

Head bent, the man shuffled through the sand to the rowboat. He shoved the boat into the water, waded a few feet, and climbed inside. Grabbing the oars, he rowed out to sea.

Eric exchanged the camera for his binoculars. After a few minutes, he announced, "Okay, he's back aboard the purse seiner."

Meg breathed a sigh of relief. "Do you think the other man went to the cave we found?"

"No." Eric lowered the binoculars. "They weren't gone long enough."

"Then maybe another entrance to the cave is on this side."

"Or another cave. But, since we don't know for sure what happened to the other guy or when he might come back, we need to get going."

A few minutes later, having retrieved their rowboat from its hiding place, they were underway. Moonlight cast a silver glow over the dark water, and the air had cooled. Meg turned to look at the mountaintop. She watched for a couple minutes, but the peak remained dark. She sighed. "The light's gone."

Eric nodded and dipped the oars into the water. "I'm betting the light was a signal to the fishing boat."

"So, someone was smuggled ashore. Maybe they were illegals." She frowned. "But only one stayed. Why smuggle only one person? Seems a waste of time and effort when other ways exist to get groups of people into the country. I've read that illegals are hidden in semi trucks or freighter containers."

"You've got a point. But maybe the individual is someone important, like a scientist or a high official of a foreign country. So he gets special treatment."

Meg wrapped her arms around her knees and massaged the spot the man had kicked. "I haven't heard of anyone defecting lately."

"We've been isolated from the news here on the island." Eric gazed out to sea as he tugged on the oars.

"True." Meg wrinkled her forehead. "But what about those two we saw the first night?"

"Yeah, the ones Laureen and Jones said were kids who came to party. They could've been lying."

Meg sat back and shoved her hands in her jacket pockets. "I have no problem believing Jones lies, but Laureen? She's gruff sometimes, but I don't think she's a bad person."

Eric pressed his lips together. "You're too trusting, Meg. Think about your wolf totem. Sometimes good, sometimes evil."

She raised her eyebrows. "Am I making a mistake, then, by trusting you?"

His eyes were solemn in the moonlight. "No, not at all. I'm the one person here you *can* trust."

****

"Hard to believe we made the entire trip without meeting Burke or Jones," Meg said when at last she stood beside Eric on the boat dock.

Eric wrapped the rowboat's line around a dock cleat. "We were lucky tonight. I hope they aren't lurking and spying on us. If we're confronted, at least we have a chance to offer up an excuse."

At Wolf House, Meg turned down her walk. "You don't have to see me to the door."

He laid a hand on her arm. "Why don't we go to my place and have a drink before we call it a night. I have Scotch, remember? I can entertain with class."

"Thanks, but I'm not much of a Scotch drinker."

"Okay, I have beer."

"I'm really not in the mood for a drink." *And being alone with you is dangerous.*

"Then what can I tempt you with?" He flashed a teasing grin. "Oh, I know—"

She put out a hand. "Let's not go there, Eric."

He shook his head. "One of these days, Meg, you'll go there. I just hope I'm the one you're with."

What an insufferable man. Meg huffed as she stepped inside her cottage. And yet, she had to admit a bit of envy, too, at Eric's casual attitude toward lovemaking. Maybe casual was the way to be; maybe that way, a person didn't get hurt.

****

"We'll know in a minute if we got anything." Eric punched the computer's keyboard.

Meg leaned forward to focus on the screen eager to see the photos of their trip to the other side of the island. "I sure hope so."

They were supposed to be working on Carl's collection, as usual, but instead Eric had downloaded the photos to Meg's computer. The first shot appeared on the screen. Eric rubbed his chin. "Hmm, not too bad."

She studied the grainy image of the fishing boat against the horizon. Two more photos showed the boat approaching the shore. A fourth blossomed on the screen.

Eric pointed to a spot on the picture "Hey, I think we've got something here. Does the name on the bow of the boat appear to be 'Alice'?"

"I don't know." Meg squinted at the screen. "Maybe. Can you make the picture bigger still?"

Eric pressed the computer's keys, using the software program's magnifying tool to enlarge the boat's bow. "Looks like 'Alice' to me."

"Me, too."

Another photo appeared.

"The two men getting out of the rowboat," Eric said. "And there's the one pointing at our footprints in the sand. Their hats hide both their faces, though, which is disappointing."

Eric was right—in every picture, the men's heads were bent and their caps pulled low over their faces. The only difference between the two was that one was considerably taller than the other. The last photo showed the second man returning to the boat. "He's the tall guy," Meg commented. "The shorter man was the one who stayed on the island."

"Yes, but that still doesn't tell us much."

They scanned all the photos again. In one, the shorter man's jacket sleeve stretched well above his wrist.

Meg widened her eyes. "Check the man's left wrist, just below his jacket sleeve. Is that a tattoo?"

Eric manipulated the photo to enlarge the man's arm. "I think you're right. The design appears to be writing. Maybe Arabic."

"Do you understand Arabic? I don't."

"I know a few words. But this image is too blurry to make out."

They looked at all the photos a third time, but they found nothing else of interest. "I'll email these to my friend," Eric said, "and then delete them from both the camera and the computer."

With a heavy sigh, Meg leaned back. "The pictures don't show anything conclusive, though."

Eric punched a couple keys. "We need more evidence. I'm still waiting for someone here to tip his hand. Or her hand, as the case may be."

"We could go to Orcas and tell the police about the men from the boat. We could show them the cave with the totem pole."

"Neither proves anything illegal is going on."

Meg's head began to ache. She closed her eyes and rubbed her forehead. "Okay. But I feel so helpless and frustrated."

He put an arm around her shoulders. "We'll find proof. Have a little faith. Here's a plan. We'll wait until the potlatch is over. If nothing comes to light, then we'll get out of here. I have a couple contacts in law enforcement who will listen to my suspicions. We'll get something started."

"All right. The potlatch will be our deciding factor."

Chapter Seventeen

Meg stood in the museum's main room, watching Carl inspect the displays she and Eric had made of the artifacts. Would he approve? She glanced at Eric.

He winked and gave her a thumbs-up.

Warmth filled her, and she flashed him a smile.

"Everything looks great," Carl finally said. "You've done a good job, and the museum has become exactly what I wanted. The building and the grounds need a few finishing touches, but we're ready for an official opening."

"And when will that be?" Meg shut the sliding doors to a display case and turned the key in the lock.

"At the potlatch this coming weekend. You'll both stay, I hope." He looked from Meg to Eric. "I'd like to have your help organizing the potlatch gifts."

"I wouldn't miss it." Eric picked up an empty cardboard box and added it to the stack of boxes in a corner.

"Neither would I," Meg said, eager to help with the gifts. Perhaps they would help to reveal the island's secret.

During the following week, the island buzzed with preparations for the festivities. Jones and Burke went to Orcas for supplies and to hire helpers for Laureen. When they returned, they dug pits on the beach in which to cook the salmon.

Meg and Eric sorted and tagged the gifts Carl would present to the visiting Nootlinga Indians. The women's gifts included replicas of carved wooden boxes, colorful woven blankets, and bead bracelets. The men would receive beaded wallets and replicas of masks. Traditionally, potlatches lasted for several days, but Carl's would last only one day, with the Nootlinga arriving in the morning and leaving in the afternoon.

Carl's other guests, who would represent his tribe, arrived on Friday. A cocktail party that evening began the festivities.

Meg and Eric walked together from their cottages to the main house. Meg's nerves were on edge. She worried about the man they'd seen sneak ashore from the fishing boat. Was he still on the island? "Any special strategy tonight?" she asked Eric. Mouth set, brow furrowed, he'd not said much since they'd set out.

"Just keep your eyes and ears open. Maybe whoever is in contact with our new resident will slip and reveal something. Someone must know about him. He has to get food somehow."

"Maybe his cohort from the boat brings food."

Eric shrugged. "Maybe. But I can't believe someone here doesn't know what's going on at the mountain."

They arrived at the house and stepped onto the patio, where the guests were gathered. Strings of colored lights added a festive air, and in one corner, a four-piece combo played classical music. Meg immediately spotted Helen talking to a middle-aged man. Her blond hair sparkled under the lights, and navy blue tights and a low-cut top showed off her figure.

Helen saw them, smiled, and waved.

Meg expected her to immediately join them and claim Eric's attention, but instead she remained with the other guest.

Eric drifted off to join Carl and his actress friend, Darla.

Addie caught up with Meg. "You're looking perky. Island life must agree with you—and Eric."

Meg saw the gleam in Addie's eyes, but she refused to take the bait. "How're you doing?"

Addie shrugged. "So-so. Norm's preparing for another trip overseas, and I don't know if I want to go or stay home. There's so much packing and other stuff to do. Sometimes, the trip isn't worth all the trouble. Seen one desert, you've seen them all."

Meg's gaze strayed to Helen again, still talking to the middle-aged man. "Helen looks happy. I remember you said she was recovering from the loss of someone. Do you think she has?"

"I don't know. I haven't talked to her much lately. Carl keeps her and Kent busy."

Lester joined them. "This is ridiculous." He nodded at the table piled with the potlatch gifts. "Why Carl keeps this stupid tradition alive is beyond me."

"The potlatch is a generous gesture." Addie stuck out her chin. "Besides, it's an excuse to party."

Lester grunted and stomped off.

Addie waved her empty wineglass. "If you'll excuse me, Meg, dear, I must get a refill."

"Of course. See you later."

Meg spotted Helen and Eric standing near the swimming pool. The two had their heads together as though exchanging secrets. She attempted to read Helen's lips, but her long hair obscured her face. Meg stepped sideways, but now Eric was in the way. His deep laughter rang out.

"Helen making time with your boyfriend?" a voice behind her said.

Meg turned to see Kent, drink in hand. "I—he's not my boyfriend."

Kent raised his eyebrows. "You spend a lot of time together."

Meg huffed under her breath. Kent was as bad as Abby with his insinuations that she had a personal interest in Eric. "That's because we work together."

"Uh huh." He sipped his drink. "How's the job going, by the way?"

She smiled. "We're finished, and Carl said he's pleased with our work."

"Good for you. Eager to get back home?"

"Yes, I am." Her response was automatic. Back home to what, though? She hadn't discovered anything about Johnny and the accident, or what he meant by "under Gemini." All she had to return to was her job—and the memories. Her chest tightened. Always, the memories.

Kent moved away to talk to Norm. A couple she'd met at the previous party approached, chatted a while, and then they too drifted away.

Someone laid a hand on her shoulder. She turned. *Eric.*

"How're you doing?" he asked.

"Fine. Just fine." She kept her tone casual. "Where's Helen?"

"Carl claimed her. He wanted to show her the gifts." He nodded to the table piled with presents for the Nootlinga. "But come on, the buffet's ready. We'll get something to eat." Eric led them to the buffet table. After helping themselves to the alder-roasted salmon, an assortment of vegetables and salads, they sat at one of the many card tables scattered about the patio.

A middle-aged couple took the remaining chairs at their table.

Helen appeared, plate in hand. She drew up a chair, squeezing in the corner between Meg and Eric. Peering around her curtain of hair, she focused on Meg. "You look all relaxed and happy. Island living must agree with you."

"Oh, yes. I've really enjoyed my stay here." Meg kept her tone cheerful.

For the rest of the meal, Helen ignored her and chatted with Eric and the other couple.

After dinner, the combo switched from classical to popular songs. Laureen's helpers cleared the patio of furniture, and several couples danced.

Meg stood at the edge of the patio, idly watching and feeling nostalgic. Dancing was a pastime she and Johnny had always enjoyed.

Eric appeared, flashing a smile. "Dance?" Without waiting for a response, he took her hand and pulled her onto the patio.

At first, Meg held herself rigid, but then the temptation—the need—to be close won out. She leaned into him and slid her hand from his shoulder to the back of his neck, threading her fingers through the ends of his hair. She closed her eyes and let a smile form on her lips.

"How are you holding up?"

His warm breath in her ear sent little shivers down her spine, but his question snapped her mind back to the present. "Fine."

"I hope so." He steered them around another couple. "We have a big day tomorrow."

Meg sniffed. "I know. I can take care of myself."

He drew away and studied her before pulling her back into his arms. "Really? I wonder about that."

"Please don't worry about me. I'm not your concern." They'd be parting soon—for good.

"Hey, don't go all independent on me now. We're in this together." He spread his hand at her lower back. "And don't go to your cottage alone tonight. Wait until I'm with you."

Meg stiffened. "Why? The man who came ashore the other night has nothing to do with me."

"Shhh." With deft moves, he guided them to the edge of the patio. "He might have something to do with Johnny. Or Norrie. Have you forgotten about them?"

"No," she said in a small voice. But, in truth, she had. She'd been so lost in his arms and the dance that she'd put aside their quest. She was really in a bad way.

The song ended, but instead of letting her go, he kept his arm around her waist. "Why don't we call it a night now? I'll walk you to your cottage."

Perhaps leaving now was a good idea. She'd never been one to party much, and she was tired. "All right.

They made the trip in silence. When she opened the door to her cottage, she expected him to follow her inside. Or at least ask. "I'll say goodnight now," he said instead. "I have things I need to do."

After shutting the door behind him, Meg paced the living room. Finally, she climbed the stairs to the loft. At the sound of voices, she went to the window and peeked out.

Several guests were heading down the path to the other cottages. Eric was not among them.

She undressed and went to bed. She tossed and turned for a while, but fatigue finally won, and she drifted off to sleep.

Sometime later, Meg awoke with a start to find a shadowy figure at her bedside. She opened her mouth to scream, but her mouth was covered by a hand.

"Shhh! It's me. Eric."

Yes, the intruder was Eric. She recognized his voice. She tugged his hand from her mouth. "What's wrong? Why are you here?"

"Checking to make sure you're okay."

Meg leaned up on her elbows. Her eyes adjusted and she could make out his features. "Why wouldn't I be?"

"When I passed by on the way to my cottage, I thought to make sure your door was locked. Gotta admit, you were a little spacey when we left the party. Anyway, your door wasn't locked, which worried me. So, I came in. Like I said, didn't mean to wake you."

"I thought I locked the door." She ran a hand over her forehead. Actually, she couldn't remember; Eric had preoccupied her.

He sat on the edge of the bed. "But you're okay."

His nearness spelled danger. She drew up the covers to her chin. "Are you sure you're not here to see if I'll let you—" Unsure how to finish the thought, she clamped shut her jaw.

"Stay the night?" He grinned. "Okay, I wouldn't turn down the offer, if you made it. But you won't. No, believe it or not, I wanted to make sure you're okay. We don't know what the new guy on the island is up to."

"You're right," she said, calmer now. "But I'm fine, and you can leave." She hugged her arms and looked away, waiting to feel the mattress shift.

Long seconds passed, and then finally, he rose. "I'll make sure I lock the door."

"Eric—"

He stopped. "Yeah?"

Ignoring the gleam in his eye, she mustered a smile. "Thanks…for checking on me."

"Sure." He waved a hand. "Any time. See you tomorrow." He turned and went down the stairs. A couple seconds later, the front door opened and then slammed shut.

Meg settled under the covers again, but sleep was a long time coming.

****

When morning came, Meg crawled out of bed, went into the bathroom, and splashed her face with cold water. Leaning into the mirror, she squinted at her image. Her eyes were slightly red-rimmed from lack of sleep. Otherwise, she looked the same as always. The events of the previous evening tumbled across her mind. She pushed away the troubling thoughts. She needed to focus on today, and the potlatch, and the museum's official opening.

She dressed and left the cottage. At the main house, enticing aromas drifted from the open dining room door. Her stomach rumbled, and her taste buds were ready for the first cup of coffee. As expected, she found a lavish breakfast buffet on the sideboard.

Many of the guests were already there, some looking perky and others dragging from the effects of last night's partying.

Meg filled a plate with scrambled eggs and toast and sat at the table. She watched for Eric, but he didn't appear. Neither did Helen. So what? Several other guests hadn't arrived yet, either. And hadn't she promised herself she would quit worrying about those two?

Shortly after breakfast, Carl told them to assemble on the beach, where they would greet their Nootlinga Indian guests from the mainland. Meg dutifully joined the crowd. Burke and Jones lit the fire in the fire pit, and the pungent smell of alder wood filled the air.

Eric finally appeared, trudging across the beach, binoculars and camera hanging around his neck. He came to stand beside her. "You look chipper this morning. After last night, I would've thought—"

She held up a hand. "Never mind last night. Let's focus on today."

He studied her, eyebrows raised. "Right. And, stick close to me. We want to be ready for whatever happens."

"They're here!" someone shouted.

Meg shaded her eyes and looked out to sea. Several longboats with blue and yellow carvings on the sides rode the waves. The dozen oarsmen on each boat dipped their oars with practiced unison and precision. Many wore conical reed hats and striped woven ponchos similar to those she and Eric had catalogued in the museum.

Cameras held by those on the shore clicked and whirred. At one end of the crowd, professional photographers recorded the event with video cameras on tripods.

Wearing a cloak of shredded cedar bark and a helmet carved in the shape of a gull's head, Carl stood in front of the group. His tanned face glowed. This was his big moment.

The longboats reached the shore, and the Nootlinga climbed out. They pulled their boats to safety from the incoming tide and then gathered together on the beach.

"Welcome, honored guests." Carl clasped his hands together and made a slight bow. "We have a big day planned. But first, a token of our friendship." He gestured to the table piled high with gifts and then nodded to Burke and Jones, who stood nearby.

Burke and Jones each picked up a basket full of the trinkets and distributed them among the newcomers.

As the Indians received their gifts, they called out their thanks and appreciation.

Carl beamed and nodded.

A Nootlinga man in his fifties, with a weathered yet handsome face, stepped forward. He wore a shirt and leggings and a cloth cloak with designs in bold shades of yellow and blue. Seashells decorated his carved wooden hat. Standing tall, he gave a response to Carl's welcome.

"I've seen him before," Eric whispered to Meg, "when I visited Norrie at the res."

"He's the chief?"

"Yeah. He seems like a decent guy, if a bit of a blowhard."

"Then he fits right in." She grinned. "Bragging is what a potlatch is all about, isn't it?"

Eric laughed. "True enough."

More speeches and singing and dancing followed, with time out for feasting on the alder-smoked salmon, roasted potatoes, and coleslaw Laureen and her crew prepared.

The afternoon was less formal, with tours of the museum and casual conversations or just relaxing. Later that afternoon, Carl assembled everyone at the beach again. Meg and Eric stood with the other guests waiting to see what their host had planned.

"Now comes the highlight of our day," Carl said. "I have something very special to present to our esteemed friends." He turned toward the embankment, cupped his hands around his mouth, and called, "Burke! Jones!"

The mini tractor Meg and Eric had seen before rumbled out of the woods. Jones was at the wheel. Burke sat in the back, keeping an eye on the long, canvas-wrapped object they towed.

Meg craned her neck. "What can that be?"

"Check the eagle carving sticking out the end," Eric said with a jerk of his chin. "Look familiar?"

Meg stared. "The totem we saw in the mountain's cave?"

"That's what I'm thinking."

Jones steered the tractor down the slope to the beach, stopping where the asphalt path ended and where a pulley apparatus had been erected. Enlisting the help of several guests, they used the pulley to upright the pole and then attached it to wires anchored in the ground.

Carl stood in front of the totem. "Dear friends of the Nootlinga, here is your long-lost totem." He addressed the others. "As you may know, the Nootlinga migrated from Canada to Puget Sound. This ancestral pole was lost to them, living on only in story and song.

"On one of my trips to the wilds of Canada, I was

lucky enough to come across the pole in the possession of a family of farmers. The pole had come with the property, which, as research showed, originally belonged to the Nootlinga. I negotiated with the owner to purchase the pole. I brought it here and, keeping it carefully hidden, restored it myself, so I could present it to you today."

Eric exchanged a glance with Meg. "So, we were right in guessing Carl was working on the pole."

"Yes." Meg nodded. "We just didn't know why."

Carl gestured to the pole. "As you can see, the totem has been fully restored and painted in the Nootlinga colors of blue, yellow, and black. At the top sits the proud eagle, your tribe's most important totem symbol."

The crowd applauded and cheered. The Nootlinga chief approached and shook Carl's hand. The two men joined the others gathering around the totem.

Eric's shoulders sagged. "I'm disappointed. All our trouble over a totem pole to give to the Nootlinga."

Meg nodded. "Looks like we've reached a dead end."

"Maybe not." Eric straightened. "Don't forget about the man who came ashore."

But Meg's spirits had hit a new low. Maybe the time had come to give up discovering what happened to Johnny and Alyssa. Maybe she needed to go home.

Chapter Eighteen

When everyone had admired the totem, they assembled on the beach for the native dancers' final performance. The guests sat on blankets or benches or on the scattered driftwood logs. Eric guided Meg to a log apart from the others, and they settled down to watch the performance.

The Indians' dance told the story of the first Nootlinga and how their totem symbols were chosen. The intricate patterns fascinated Meg, and the steady drum rhythms resonated pleasantly in her ears.

When the dance was over, Carl and the Indian chief gave farewell speeches. Afterward, the Indians headed for their longboats and their journey back to the mainland. For now, the totem Carl had given them would stay on the island. He promised to deliver it to the reservation in the near future.

The dancers were the last to climb into the boats. One of the men caught Meg's attention.

She shaded her eyes against the sun and squinted. Sure enough, on his left wrist was a tattoo. Her pulse quickened, and she nudged Eric with her elbow. "Check out the dancer wearing the blue and yellow helmet through your binoculars."

Eric raised his binoculars. "Okay, what about him?"

"Look at his left wrist."

"Whoa, I see what you mean. The tattoo."

Meg clutched her purse strap. "Isn't he the same guy who came ashore?"

He lowered the binoculars and met her gaze. "Judging by that one identification, I'd say he is."

"So they're smuggling him to the mainland?"

"Looks that way. Time for us to blow the whistle."

"How? He's getting away." She returned her attention to the Indians in time to see the tattooed man climb into the boat.

"I'll show you. But first, is there anything you want from your cottage? We may not be coming back. No baggage, though. That would be sure to set off an alarm."

Meg's pulse beat so hard she could barely think. "Ah, no, I guess not."

"Then let's go." He grabbed her hand. "Walk normal. We don't want to attract attention."

They strolled across the beach and up the embankment. Once they were out of sight of the others, they ran—through the woods, past their cottages and onto a path leading to the beach. "I hid a boat," Eric said, "and this is the time to use it."

"You think of everything."

He laughed. "I try to."

They reached the shore. Meg helped Eric pull a motorboat from the bushes and push it toward the water.

"Hold it right there!"

Meg whirled to see Jones running toward them. Her breath caught.

He held a gun, pointed directly at them. "Stay where you are!" Jones commanded.

Eric slowly straightened. "Do what he says, Meg."

Meg marveled at how calm Eric appeared, while she fought down panic with every breath.

"Now shove the boat into the water," Jones said.

Like a bull ready to charge, Eric's brow furrowed and his head lowered.

This is not the time for a male ego standoff, she wanted to shout but bit back the words.

"Do it!" Jones yelled. "Or she gets it." He shifted the gun toward Meg.

Eric raised his hands. "Okay, okay."

Meg tugged on the rope tied to the boat's bow, and Eric pushed from the stern. The boat slid from the sand and into the water.

Jones stepped forward. "Push the boat way out and let it go."

Eric gave the boat a shove.

Meg let the rope slip from her fingers and, with a sinking heart, watched their means of escape drift away.

"I know yer carryin', Richards, so get rid of it."

Eric's lips tightened, but he reached to his hip.

"Easy now," Jones warned and squared his stance. "Don't ferget I got her covered."

Meg glanced at Jones' gun pointed at her and shivered. She'd no doubt he would shoot if his command wasn't obeyed. Then she would never find out what happened to Johnny and Alyssa.

Keeping his gaze focused on Jones, Eric slowly pulled out his gun.

"Toss it in the water."

Eric threw the gun. The weapon arced high, hit the water with a plop, and sank.

"Cell next," Jones commanded.

Eric growled, but he took his cell phone from his belt and threw it in the water.

Jones sneered. "You're a real good boy." He looked at Meg. "The purse around your neck—toss it."

Meg slipped off her purse and clutched it, loathe to lose her ID, cell phone, and several photos of Alyssa, tucked away in a hidden pocket. But what was she to do, with Jones holding a gun on them? Gritting her teeth, she threw the purse into the water.

"You got anything in your pockets?" Jones asked. "A phone, a gun?"

"My phone was in my purse." She gestured to the spot where the purse had landed, spreading rings as it sank. "I don't carry a gun."

"You better be tellin' the truth. I find out different later, you ain't gonna like what happens. Now you two get in front of me and start walking."

"Where to?" Eric stood his ground.

"Through the woods."

Eyebrows high, Eric shot a glance inland. "To Mt. Gemini? Why?"

"Shut up and get going!"

Eric glowered but he reached for Meg's hand.

She grasped his fingers and fell into step beside him. What choice did they have? Holding that weapon, Jones owned all the power.

With Jones and his gun at their backs, they left the beach behind and entered the woods. The sunlight vanished and the temperature dropped. Eventually, the asphalt gave way to dirt paths. The vegetation thickened, and a damp, earthy smell filled the air.

Meg wished she and Eric could end this madness, but they dared not try anything. Not now, anyway.

They reached the mountain. Jones led them to the spot where Meg and Eric had seen the men come ashore. Keeping his gun trained on them, he pushed aside bushes to reveal a crude hole in the mountain's side. Jones nodded at the hole. "Get in!"

Eric glowered.

"Just do it!" Jones took a step toward Meg.

Muttering under his breath, Eric ducked his head and entered the opening.

Her heart pounding, Meg crept in behind him. The cave was twice as large as the one in which they'd found the totem. Like that cave, crude lumber shored up the sides and the ceiling. A cot covered with a sleeping bag stood against one wall. Next to the cot, a small table held a lantern and a radio.

What would happen now? Would Jones leave them here? The smell already made her gag, and the thought of being held prisoner in this hole sent chills spiraling down her spine.

The underbrush outside rustled, and a shadow darkened the doorway. Someone stooped to enter the cave and then stood erect.

"You've got them?" the newcomer said, as he stepped farther into the cave.

Kent Gheller. Meg gasped then hastily covered her mouth.

"Got 'em," Jones growled.

Eric leaped forward and thrust his nose into Kent's face. "I've got everything figured out now. You're not smuggling drugs, you're smuggling terrorists."

Kent shrugged and shoved him away. "We do a little of everything. Too bad you had to come nosing around." He turned to Meg. "Why couldn't you just accept Johnny's death as an accident?"

Meg stared. "You know who I am?"

"Of course."

His voice dripped with scorn.

"Then why did you hire me?"

"To keep an eye on you."

The pieces to the puzzle fell into place. She wrapped her arms around her stomach. "And so you could search our house in Seattle, and my cottage here."

Kent shrugged. "We had to make sure Johnny didn't leave any evidence."

"So he found out about you," Eric said.

Kent's lips thinned. "And thought he could blackmail us. Stupid man. And you." He pointed at Eric. "You're here because of the girl, Norrie."

Eric's eyes narrowed. "She learned what you were doing, too. Just like Johnny did."

Kent only smiled.

"Why you—you bastard!" Letting out a growl, Eric lunged at Kent.

Jones leaped between the two men and punched Eric in the jaw.

Eric staggered backward several steps. A moment later, he recovered and swung at Jones. "I've got a score to settle with you!" He grabbed Jones' wrist. The gun wavered wildly. The two men continued to wrestle until Kent stepped forward and kicked Eric in the back of his knee. With a groan, Eric let go of Jones and crumpled to the ground.

Meg gasped and took a step toward Eric.

Kent caught her arm. "No more fighting!"

Jones backed away but kept his gun trained on Eric.

Eric staggered to his feet. He glowered at Jones and rubbed his jaw.

"Why, Kent?" Meg wanted to stall for time, hoping Eric would develop a plan, but she needed answers, too. "Why are you a traitor to your country?"

Kent curled his lip. "The U.S. is not my country. I have allegiance to no one but myself. Besides, you Americans think you can rule the world with your armies. You think you can invade a country any time you please and bomb the hell out of it."

"That's what happened in Sukarla, isn't it?" Eric narrowed his gaze. "Where your wife's from."

Kent shook his fist at Eric. "Yes! All her family murdered by a bomb the Americans set off. A mistake, they said. They didn't mean to harm innocent people. They just wanted to get rid of the dictator. And for what reason? Because they didn't like him."

"But not all Americans believe the same way." Meg spread her hands. "Sometimes we don't like what our government does, but we can do nothing. Killing Eric and me will be just as wrong as what happened in your wife's country. Does that make sense?"

"'An eye for an eye' makes sense to me. You Americans need to learn a lesson. But enough talk." He reached into his jacket pocket, took out a pouch, and from that produced a hypodermic needle.

Frowning, Jones stared at the needle. "What's that for?"

"A little something to keep them quiet until we finish our job."

Jones waved his gun. "Whyn't I finish 'em off now?"

"No, you already screwed up enough. We do it my

way. We leave them here until I bring some other evidence I want to get rid of. Then we close up the hole."

"Yeah." Jones grinned. "Their boat's already adrift. Everybody'll think they had an accident."

"Like when you and Burke tried to ram our boat during the storm?" Eric spread his feet apart.

Jones chuckled. "Just havin' a little fun."

"Shut up, Jones!" Kent demanded. "You talk too much. We need to get on with this. We'll take care of Mr. Richards first. Cover her, Jones." Holding out the needle, he strode to Eric.

Jones grabbed Meg and shoved the gun against her head.

The cold barrel pressed into her skull. Her throat went dry, and her heart hammered. These men had murdered Johnny and her precious daughter. And Eric's friend, Norrie. Would she and Eric die, too, without bringing them to justice?

Kent closed the gap between him and Eric.

Bracing himself, Eric took a swing but missed Kent because he ducked.

Kent straightened and, arm outstretched, plunged the needle into Eric's shoulder.

Eric's eyes widened. He staggered a few steps, and then closed his eyes and slumped to the ground.

Meg gasped and clutched her stomach.

Kent kicked Eric's side. "Stupid bastard." He looked at Meg, his eyes narrowing, as he advanced. "Your turn." He grabbed her arm and plunged the needle into her flesh.

Pain arrowed through Meg, followed by a pressure along her veins when the drug traveled its course.

Blackness framed and then filled her vision. She struggled to keep her thoughts straight, but staying alert was impossible. She finally gave in and crumpled to the dirt floor.

****

"Meg! Wake up! Wake up!"

Leave me alone. Let me sleep. Let me die.

"Meg! You've got to wake up!"

Meg opened her eyes and spotted a man bent over her. "E-Eric? Is that you?"

"Yep, it's me, and we need to get out of here."

"Out of...where?" She squinted into the dim light. "Oh...the...cave.

Eric grasped Meg's arms and pulled her to a sitting position.

"I'm so—so d-dizzy." She ran a shaky hand over her forehead.

"C'mon outside."

With Eric's help, she managed to stand, and together they stumbled out the cave's opening. Meg gulped in the cool air. "Yes, b-better now."

Body tensed, Eric gazed around. "We gotta get out of here before Kent and Jones come back. They won't spare us next time."

"But we l-lost our boat."

"I'll get another one. We'll find a place for you to hide until I come for you."

Alone? Meg gripped his arm. "No. I'll go with you."

Eric briefly closed his eyes and took a deep breath. "Okay, but if you can't keep up, you'll have to wait. Understand?"

"I'll keep up." More awake now, she peered at

him. "How'd you recover so fast?"

He grinned and pantomined. "I jerked my arm so Kent's needle only grazed me, and most of the drug soaked my shirt sleeve. Then I faked it. But, come on, let's get a move on."

The bushes behind them rustled.

"Someone's coming!" Meg's heart hammered.

Eric whirled. "Who—?"

Helen burst from the bushes.

Meg stared at her disheveled appearance. Her hair was in tangles and dirt stained her white T-top and slacks. "Helen?"

"What are *you* doing here?" Eric propped his hands on his hips

"I came to..." Helen pressed her stomach and gasped for breath. "To help you. C'mon, hurry. There's a boat...at the beach."

"Why should we believe you?" Meg's stomach knotted, and she moved closer to Eric.

"You just have to. Please, hurry!" Helen beckoned.

Eric looked toward the water and then at Helen. "All right, show us where the boat is."

Meg still wasn't sure she trusted Helen, but she was too weak to argue. She fell into step beside Eric, and they followed Helen through the underbrush.

The group soon reached the water. Meg let out a relieved breath when she saw a motorboat on the beach tied to a log. But why was Helen helping them? Because she was in love with Eric? Meg rubbed her forehead. She was still too drugged to figure this out.

The three of them shoved the boat into the water. Eric held out his hand to Meg. Meg took a step toward him but then stopped and turned to Helen. "Why are you helping us?"

Helen twisted her hands together. "Because I don't want your murders on my conscience. All I wanted was…" She bit her lip and looked away. "All I wanted was Johnny."

Meg dropped her jaw. Was her ex-husband Helen's lost love? "Johnny? You and Johnny?"

Helen hugged her waist. "I was in love with him, but he was still in love with you." Bitterness crept into her voice.

"Kent and his allies killed Johnny." Eric gripped the boat against a wave breaking over the bow. "And my friend's daughter, Norrie."

"I know." Helen nodded. "I thought Johnny's death was an accident. But today I overheard Kent and Jones talking about how they met Johnny in a bar that night. Johnny thought they were ready to pay him off for keeping quiet about their money laundering, but instead they drugged his coffee, hoping he'd get in an accident on the way home. I hate Kent for killing Johnny." Tears rolled down her cheeks.

"Oh, Helen, I didn't know…" So much tragedy. Meg held out her hand and took a step toward the distraught woman.

Helen shook her head and backed away. "Just get out of here before it's too late."

"You need to get away, too." Eric extended his hand. "Come with us."

"No. I'll be okay. Don't worry about me."

Meg and Eric soon were underway. Sitting in the stern, Meg looked back at the island. Helen stood on the beach where they'd left her. Meg waved, and Helen waved back. A lump formed in Meg's throat. She kept her gaze on the woman until they rounded a corner of the island and she was lost from view.

Meg turned her attention to the trip ahead. "Where are we going?"

"To Orcas." Eric barely looked up from steering the boat. "It's the nearest place to get help."

On the open water, Meg feared they would encounter the Nootlinga longboats or other boats from Gemini, whose occupants might recognize them, but the only other craft to cross their path were a couple of sailboats.

Reaching Orcas seemed to take forever, but at last, they pulled up to the public dock. Fifteen minutes later, they sat in the police station, telling their story to the island authorities.

Chapter Nineteen

Seattle, one month later

Eric added one more item to the specs for his client's new office network, and then closed the file and shut down his computer. He sat back and clasped his hands behind his head. His life had returned to normal, more or less. He was home running his business and working for the FBI.

Keeping his mind in the present proved difficult, though, when Gemini still occupied his thoughts. Thankfully, he and Meg had reached the Orcas Island authorities in time for them to intercept the Nootlinga's return trip to their Washington reservation. The terrorist aboard was taken into custody. At the same time, more cops went to Gemini, and, much to Carl's and everyone else's shock, arrested Kent Gheller and Jones.

Eric chuckled, imagining the look on Carl's face when he heard how his trusted employee had been using his island.

Bit by bit, the story came together. An ambitious plot, too. The terrorists planned to simultaneously blow up monuments and landmarks around the country. In addition to Seattle's Space Needle, they'd targeted Las Vegas' MGM Grand Hotel, St. Louis' Gateway Arch, Washington D.C.'s Lincoln Memorial, and Houston, Texas' Astrodome. The crudely drawn maps he found on Gemini were of the various targets.

Other terrorists had already been smuggled into the U.S. at points along the U.S.-Canadian border. The two men he and Meg saw their first night on Gemini were also part of the plot. From Gemini, they traveled to Nevada to handle the Las Vegas detonation.

Eric's gaze fell on the framed photo of Norrie sitting on his desk, and his chest tightened. He picked up the photo and looked into her dark eyes. "We got 'em," he whispered.

Jones had confessed Norrie overheard him and another tribal member talking about terrorists hidden on Gemini and threatened to blow the whistle. So, they'd killed her with an overdose.

"Yeah, we got 'em"—he said again, as he replaced the photo—"but I'd give anything to have you back." He wouldn't forget her, ever. To make sure her memory lived for others, he'd established a fund in her name to help other drug-addicted kids through rehab. Both he and Meg were called in to the Bureau's office to tell their stories.

Of course, now she knew the truth about his association with the FBI. She didn't seem surprised or upset that he hadn't confided in her.

Thinking their meeting at the Bureau would end their association, he'd said goodbye. But he couldn't get her out of his mind. Weeks had passed, but he wanted to see her. Even more, he wanted to *be with* her, to be the kind of guy who could do the relationship thing. If seeing the shrink would help him to get his act together, he'd do that, too.

Since he returned, he hadn't seen Sally Marshall. They spoke on the phone a couple times, but neither suggested getting together. He needed to talk to Sally now and set things straight. He picked up his phone and soon had her on the line. "Hey, Sally. It's Eric. Been a while."

"Oh, Eric…I'm glad you called. I've been wanting to talk."

Eric leaned forward. "Is something wrong? Your voice sounds funny."

"No, I'm okay. But I've met someone and…"

"And fell in love?" Maybe this would be easier than he'd anticipated.

"Yes, that's exactly what happened."

"Good for you, Sally." *And good for me, too.*

"You really think so? I was worried about telling you."

Eric picked up a stray paperclip and dropped it in the clip holder. "Hey, you know our arrangement was just friends. We never were serious."

"I know, but still…"

"Don't worry about me." Eric smiled to himself. "I've met someone, too."

"Really? You're not just saying that to make me feel better?"

She sounded more cheerful now. "I'm telling the truth. Honest."

"Are you getting married?"

He laughed. "That kind of commitment is w-a-ay down the road. But how about you?"

"Next month. I'll send you an invitation."

"Great. I'll be there." Eric punched off the call, smiling. Sally was a great person, and he wished her all the best.

But now, the time had come to get on with his life.

After taking a deep breath, he picked up the phone again.

****

"Here are examples of newsletters my other clients have produced." Meg opened a notebook and slid it across the table toward her new client, Jessica Forrester.

Jessica paged through the notebook. "These are really nice."

"They are," Meg agreed, unable to keep the pride from her tone. "And I can give you the templates for any, or all of them, and show you how to set up your service online."

Jessica frowned and brushed a lock of gray hair from her forehead. "You really think I can do this computer stuff?"

"I do." Meg leaned back in her chair. "Look at all the experience you've had working for your ex-husband's construction firm. Plus, you already have one company lined up."

"Right. But I'll need a lot more."

"Don't worry. I can help with that, too."

After Jessica left, Meg checked her wristwatch. Almost lunch time. She'd make notes on her meeting and then have a bite to eat. She sat at the computer, but, as often was the case, her mind wandered to Gemini Island. She'd been relieved to know Carl Miller wasn't part of the terrorist organization. He really was a decent guy, if a bit full of himself.

Wanting to hear more of her story, Meg agreed to Helen's request to get together a week or so ago.

"I need to apologize for my big come-on to Eric," Helen had said over coffee at a local restaurant. "Oh, he's a very handsome guy, but I wasn't really interested. I wanted to make you jealous. Johnny told me that when you two were together, you were jealous sometimes."

"I was," Meg admitted. "I seem to have a problem that way."

"And I was bitter and angry when he told me he would reconcile if you'd agree. Then when he was killed..." She lowered her gaze. "I had nothing, not even the hope that he would change his mind and want me. I didn't want you to be happy, either, so I played up to Eric. Stupid of me, and I'm truly sorry."

Meg's heart went out to the woman. "Oh, Helen, I'm sorry, too. Sorry for both of us. I do have a problem with jealousy. And, although this may sound strange, I'm glad you churned it up, because I've decided to get professional advice. But most of all, you saved our lives. I'll always be grateful to you."

When she and Helen said good-bye, if not exactly friends, they were at least on better terms than before.

At last, Meg had closure on Johnny and Alyssa's deaths. She was still grieving, of course, and would be for a long time. Did a parent ever truly recover from the loss of a child? She didn't think so. An ache would always live in her heart for her beloved Alyssa.

Her thoughts turned to Eric. She hadn't seen him since they'd been questioned at the FBI office. His role as an agent hadn't really surprised her. She understood why he hadn't confided in her and held no grudge. If only she could forget him, but she couldn't. Why? They had no unfinished business. They'd had a common goal, but once the goal was reached, no reason remained for them to see each other. Still, she kept reliving the times they'd spent together. Being with him had made her feel so alive.

Her ringing cell phone interrupted her troubled musings. She picked up the phone, expecting the caller to be a client.

Instead an all-too-familiar voice said, "Hello, Meg."

Her heart skipped a beat. "Eric?"

"Yeah, it's me. How're you doing?"

Meg absently smoothed her hair. "Fine. I'm back at work."

"Me, too. Nothing like routine to put stability in your life."

"Right." She tightened her grip on the phone. "Why are you calling? Did we leave loose ends with the Gemini investigation?"

He laughed. "As a matter of fact, a loose end does exist."

"Oh?"

"Yeah—us."

"Us?" Her throat tightened. She wanted to use the cliché, "There is no 'us'" but bit back the words.

"Look, Meg, how about getting together tomorrow for lunch? It's Saturday. You do take off the weekends, don't you?"

Meg's throat went dry. "Ah, usually."

"So? Tomorrow? How about the Space Needle? We saved it, didn't we? We should celebrate by having lunch there."

His choice of location was perfect. Meg had to smile. "I agree. We should celebrate."

"Great. Meet you by the elevator at eleven-thirty."

Meg ended the call excited but full of misgivings, too. Could they meet as friends? Or would she only be stirring up feelings better left alone? What if he wanted to have a relationship? Was she ready?

****

Sitting across from Eric at a window table in the Space Needle's revolving restaurant, Meg gazed at Elliot Bay, where a variety of boats plied water so calm only a few ripples broke the surface. "The view here is breathtaking."

"It is," Eric agreed as he leaned forward. "But so is the view across the table. Good to see you again, Meg."

"Good to see you, too, Eric." All too true, given how handsome he looked in a navy blue shirt and slacks and with his hair neatly trimmed. Seeing him today made her realize how much she'd missed him.

Their meals arrived. Meg ordered the baked halibut and Eric opted for steak. They talked about their respective businesses, stopping now and then to point out the sights as the restaurant moved on its slow rotation. Meg showed him her apartment building on Queen Anne Hill. A glimpse of the Olympic Mountains prompted him to relate a hiking adventure.

After they finished eating, they took the elevator to the ground floor. She wondered if their time together was about to end. Did she want it to?

But he caught her hand and drew her aside. "Got time to wander around the Center for a while?"

"I do. I cleared my calendar for the afternoon."

He grinned. "So did I."

They strolled one of the many walkways that threaded the grounds. They passed a couple clowns juggling colored balls, and a group of street musicians playing ragtime tunes. Eric pulled a few bills from his pocket and tossed them into the musicians' open violin case. From there, they went to the International Fountain, a huge cement basin with water spewing from a silver dome in the center.

"So, what's in your future?" he asked after they had admired the fountain and continued on.

She cast him a covert glance. Was he only making conversation, or was something else behind his inquiry? Did she want there to be? "Just working at my business. What about you?"

Eric grasped her elbow to steer them around several children holding balloons aloft as they ran by. "Same. My software business and my work with the Bureau. But I want to do something else, too, that's very important."

His serious tone put her on alert. "Oh? What?"

"I want to spend time with you, and for us to get to know each other better."

Meg frowned. "But I thought—"

"That when we left Gemini, we'd say good-bye and never see each other again? Okay, maybe I did send that message. But I changed my mind."

"Why?"

"Geez, you ask hard questions. Because I'm in love with you."

Meg skidded to a stop. "You want us to get to know each other better *because* you're in love with me? Don't you get to know someone and fall in love in the process?"

He lifted a shoulder. "Okay, so we did it backwards. What about you? How do you feel about me?"

We? Talk about hard questions. Still, his bold confession gave her courage. "Truth is, I haven't been able to get you out of my mind."

He grinned and reached for her hand. "That's a good sign."

"I keep thinking about the times we were together."

"Yeah, we sure generated some heat, didn't we?"

"Not just *those* times. Working together in the museum, exploring the island, eating meals together. Sharing our feelings." Sharing had made her feel close to him.

"Let's sit and work this out." He drew her off the path and across the grass to a bench under a maple tree. When he'd settled her beside him, he put an arm around her shoulders. "So what do you think? About us?"

"I'm in love with you, too. I've been afraid to admit it because love is scary. And risky."

"Life is a risk. But we'll take it slow, okay? We both have issues, but I'm game if you are." He drew her close. His lips brushed her hair. "I've missed you, Meg. Missed you like crazy."

She leaned into him and buried her face against his chest, inhaling his masculine scent. "I've missed you, too."

He cupped her chin and gazed into her eyes. "Why don't we go to my place? I'll show you just how much I've missed you."

"Some of your sexual healing?" She teased, recalling how he'd tempted her when they were on the island.

"We'll see." He traced a finger down her cheek. "Nothing will happen until you're ready. But we share much more. You just said so."

"I'd like to spend time with you today—and tomorrow, too. And you know what? I just might be ready."

He laughed and covered her lips with a warm and tender kiss.

Her heart swelled with love for this very special man. She didn't know where the road they'd stepped onto would lead. They had no guarantees. But, given the love she and Eric shared, she believed they'd be traveling the road together for a long, long time.

A word about the author...

A resident of the Pacific Northwest, Linda Hope Lee writes contemporary romance, romantic suspense, and mystery novels. She also enjoys watercolor painting, photography, and collecting children's books.
www.lindahopelee.com

~~

Other Titles by the Author
Dark Memories
Finding Sara
Loving Rose
Marrying Molly